Forbidden Study

He could sense something was wrong. "Was that too much?" He was worried now, his hair falling over his forehead, looking at her with concern. "I didn't want to hurt you."

But he had wanted to, in a strange, dark way and they both knew it. Yet he hadn't hurt her. It was as though in reaching for her, in trying to take her and own her wholly, she only slipped further away.

Laura looked at him. His face, its flawless angles, which she loved. The set of his eyes and their dark grey colour. The texture of his skin, shadowed with stubble from not shaving that day.

She felt an overwhelming love for him. She rejoiced in being with him, she felt luckier than anything to be the one he had chosen. For him to feel the same way about her that she did about him.

Yet there was something else. A flash of something that she buried deep down within herself.

She smiled at him, and let him kiss her and hold her, and the world gently tipped back to where it was supposed to be.

Tempting Her Teacher

"Being this close to you is like torture. But it's wrong - I'm your teacher."

Catholic school teacher Carl Spencer faces a crisis of faith when he falls for his student Juliet, how can he resist the temptation to be with her?

Juliet, a girl with a troubled past, makes a bet that she can seduce hot new Latin teacher Mr Spencer, a devout Christian.

But while Mr Spencer wrestles with his faith as he tries to resist his growing attraction to Juliet, she's starting to realise that it's become more than just a game for her.

Summer's Edge

He's fighting it but he needs this as much as I do.

When Stewart Walker finds out the girl he kissed is a student at his school he's furious and determined to keep away. But 18-year-old Alice has fallen hard and won't give up. She wants him to teach her body and her mind, even though a relationship is strictly against the rules. He's struggling to resist the attraction despite knowing he could lose his job.

Throughout the illegal raves and festivals of Britain's summer of '92, Alice and Stewart dance closer and closer to the edge.

Available in paperback or eBook from Lulu.com

FORBIDDEN STUDY

by

Noël Cades

First Printing, 2016

ISBN: 0-9945811-1-4
ISBN-13: 978-0-9945811-1-2

To Goddess of Blah

PART I

Possessing

I've taught thee Love's sweet lesson o'er,
A task that is not learn'd with tears

Sylvia; Or, the May Queen, George Darley

1. In Calabria

It was three weeks since Laura had seen Mr Rydell on the last day of term: three weeks of cold, dark days and feeling his absence like a physical pain.

Now she was leaving the grey English winter behind for southern Italy. Where she would be with him once again.

Charlotte sat next to Laura on the plane, both of them clipping in their belts having just watched the safety demonstration. An air hostess offered them a small carton of water or orange juice and they both chose the juice.

Laura hadn't flown very often and her stomach and legs felt weirdly giddy. She sipped the juice slowly through the thin straw: it was cold and very sweet.

It was amazing that they had both been allowed to fly out together for a week's holiday, but Susie had worked her magic. She'd arranged for her uncle to send the invitation himself, drafted on some official notepaper that made it look like a royal summons. Even Charlotte's strict father had been impressed enough to accept it.

"Are you excited? You must be dying to see him," Charlotte said.

"Terrified." But Laura was thrilled as well. They hadn't even been able to phone easily because of her parents being there. Even Christmas had felt flat, though she had tried to hide this from her family.

"It's a pity Margery couldn't come."

It was rather that Margery wouldn't come not that she was unable to travel. Her own father, a modern languages teacher, would have been delighted for her to go if it meant learning a bit of Italian. But Margery had been more scared than attracted by all Susie's wild tales about what she got up to in Italy, and felt she would be out of her depth. She got homesick easily, even at school.

So it would be just the three of them. And Mr Rydell, if he came. Laura had run through all sorts of panicked scenarios in her head where he didn't arrive or even had his plane crash. Most of all she was worried he would see her and no longer feel the same. No matter how much Charlotte tried to reassure her, Laura was sick with nerves.

Disembarking all passed in a bit of a blur of Italian voices and rummaging for passports. Charlotte was already eyeing up a customs official who looked more like a TV star than an airport worker, and getting even more of an eye back.

"We'll get arrested!" Laura warned her. "They'll think you're trying to bribe your way in."

"It's not like we need a visa," Charlotte whispered back. "God, just compare this lot to the staff at Heathrow. I wonder if he'll frisk me?"

It was hard to believe that southern Italy was actually warm and sunny at that time of year. Not hot, certainly, but when they had landed the sun was shining and it certainly didn't feel wintry as they climbed down the aeroplane steps. Now, coming outside the terminal, it definitely felt like holiday weather.

Susie met them at the airport, looking as vivacious as ever. She was accompanied by two incredibly good looking Italian men, one of whom Laura recognised from photos as Susie's cousin Ferdinando.

"Ciao!" Susie greeted them while the men helped with their suitcases, carrying them to a car parked outside the airport. She was wearing a brilliant scarlet coat that swung as she walked and looked like something Audrey Hepburn might have worn if Roman Holiday had been set in winter.

The car turned out not to be just any car, but a silver Ferrari. Laura had assumed Susie's family were well off from certain things she had mentioned, though Susie never boasted, but this was the first real sign of it. Inside it was lined with soft grey leather. Laura wasn't a huge fan of leather interiors. One of her uncles drove an expensive company car with leather seats and they were always sticky in summer against bare skin.

But she and Charlotte were both wearing jeans today, so they could revel in the luxury.

The two men had greeted Laura and Charlotte in heavily accented English, but now they were talking together in a torrent of Italian, and the girls couldn't make out a single word. This was despite having avidly studied a phrasebook in the hope of being able to exchange some basic greetings with Susie's family.

"Does your cousin speak English?" Charlotte asked.

"More or less, not very well though. Massimo is more fluent but they're both lazy about making the effort. I suppose it's good for me, as it forces me to brush up my Italian whenever I stay with them," Susie told her.

Laura had guessed that Massimo was Ferdinando's boyfriend, whom Susie had spoken of before. They both looked like models: dark, lean and dashing. Perhaps Italian men were like this generally with their Mediterranean looks. They would soon find out.

After a few miles with the three of them crammed into the back of the the sports car, which Ferdinando drove at breakneck speed through often winding country roads, climbing out of the city into a hilly district, they rolled up at the impressive gates of Susie's aunt's and uncle's house. It was fronted by huge railings adorned with lavish gilding, with white marble lions atop each pillar of the gate posts.

Susie laughed when she saw their reaction. "It's awful, isn't it? Like a mafiosa villa. Actually that's just what it was before the last owner ended up at the bottom of the sea and my uncle bought it. He wanted to tone it down but Zia Viola thought it was hilarious. They only spend the winter here anyway."

Laura knew that "zia" meant "aunt" but she wondered what they should call her. Signora, perhaps.

The two young men unloaded the cases from the car, embraced Susie and nodded to the two English girls, there was a flurry of "*a presto*" from them and attempts at "*grazie*" from Laura and Charlotte, and they were gone.

"Here we are then," Susie said. "I'll show you to your rooms. Though you probably won't be staying in yours much once lover boy arrives," she said to Laura. "I've booked him into a glorious hotel, it's all arranged."

"Won't your aunt and uncle mind?" Charlotte asked.

"Not at all. I'll just tell them whatever I like, they won't care. I often stay over with Ferdinando at Massimo's place when we all go out on the town. Or that's where they think I stay, anyway." She gave a mischievous smile and they knew they were in for a wild ride themselves as Susie's guests.

The rooms were lovely, spacious and airy and reminded Laura of a luxury hotel. There were big, thick white towels on the beds and both of them had ensuite bathrooms. She had thought they might have to share, which was fine as they were used to being all together in the dormitory at school, but the house was so large there were plenty of spare rooms.

"If you need any more towels Graziella will bring them. She's the housekeeper," Susie explained.

They were in Charlotte's room while she unpacked, catching up on news and gossip. Susie seized some schoolbooks that Charlotte had brought. "'Select Letters of Pliny' and 'Latin Exercises for Schoolboys'? Goodness I'm thankful I don't do Latin with you. Anyway you absolutely can't waste your time doing holiday work here. I'm confiscating these."

"But we won't have any time when we get back, before school starts," Charlotte said. Her father would kill her if she didn't get her holiday work done. It had been one of the conditions of being allowed to go to Italy.

"You can copy mine," Laura told her. "Have you already done all of yours?" she asked Susie.

"God no. I never do holiday work, it's supposed to be a break, after all."

As ever Susie was completely unconcerned about school rules and conventions. They simply did not matter to her. She didn't care about getting into trouble, she was fearless. Laura often envied Susie for her attitude. It must be very liberating to simply not care.

For her own part she did need to do the schoolwork they had been set. Mr Rydell had started coaching her to apply for Oxford or Cambridge, and she couldn't risk being put into lower sets when she got back. How he was going to coach her now he no longer taught at Francis Hall she wasn't sure, but she knew he intended to continue.

Her body and her mind. He was her instructor in everything, and she shivered thinking of his voice and his touch.

"You have that dreamy look again, Laura, I know exactly who you're thinking about," Charlotte said.

"He'll be here tomorrow. I wanted you both to myself today and tonight, so we could see the sights without Laura getting all lovey dovey with her man and ignoring us completely," Susie told them.

Laura protested but she knew the others were right. The minute she saw him no one else would exist. The intensity of how she felt often frightened her. It was all-consuming.

Susie took them downstairs to meet her aunt. Zia Viola was an amazingly glamorous and beautiful woman, very young-looking for her age given she had grown up sons. Her glossy dark hair fell in a long curtain, without a trace of grey. She was slender with curves in the most desirable places, just like Susie, and the clinging, dark aubergine coloured gown she was was wearing accentuated her figure. The others could easily see where Susie had inherited her looks and charm from.

Laura and Charlotte, who had travelled over in jeans and jerseys since England had been freezing, felt all the more scruffy.

Susie's aunt insisted they call her Zia and offered them drinks, alcoholic ones. She managed a little English, also heavily accented, but mainly spoke in Italian with Susie interpreting.

"Zia Viola says she hopes we'll dine with them tonight. I've told her we're all going out on the town, but things don't kick off until later anyway. Besides it's always quieter in winter."

Laura and Charlotte were completely content to go along with whatever was required of them. So long as Susie kept up the translation.

* * *

After dinner Ferdinando drove them into the town and they went to a couple of clubs. At one of them there was a short queue by

13

the door but Ferdinando and Susie simply ignored it and walked straight in. The doorman grinned at Ferdinando, clearly recognising him.

It helped that they had all dressed up. Given it was winter even in Italy, Laura and Charlotte had thought they might just wear jeans and sexy tops. But Susie got everyone into glamour mode, and even raided her aunt's wardrobe for a few pieces. Laura ended up with a silvery tunic dotted with sequins that was supposed to be worn with evening trousers, but Susie said it looked fine as a mini-dress.

At the nightclub Charlotte and Laura found themselves magnets for male attention and were constantly approached with free drinks and requests to dance.

"It's because you're so blonde and English looking," Susie told them. "You stand out a mile."

She wasn't short of admirers either and seemed to be acquainted with a lot of people in the town, as Ferdinando also was.

"What about Darius?" Charlotte asked Susie after she came back from dancing with an attractive male friend. Susie had been dating Darius, a sixth former at St Duncan's, for the past few months.

"Oh you know, we have an understanding. It's not a full on, true love forever thing like Laura and Mr Rydell. Or you and Julian, given how that appears to be going," Susie said. "Besides which I've known Bruno for years, there's nothing in it."

Charlotte had been to stay with the family of her boyfriend Julian before Christmas, though she had told her parents she was visiting Laura in Cornwall. They were used to this kind of subterfuge: going to boarding school meant you needed to be resourceful if you wanted to have fun.

"It's not that serious. Definitely nothing like Laura anyway." Charlotte nudged Laura who was gazing into space. "No need to ask what you're thinking about. I bet you're counting the actual hours until he gets here."

Laura tried to deny it but the others knew her too well.

"You should both dance. Boyfriends or not, you can't sit here like a couple of wallflowers all night," Susie told them. Charlotte

14

was quite happy to be paired off with one of Susie's handsome friends, but Laura found it hard to drum up any interest in dancing with her partner despite his own good looks.

It wasn't even that she felt guilty for dancing with another man. How could she, when every other male was meaningless compared to Mr Rydell? Though if he saw her with another guy... she shivered for a moment, remembering a similar situation.

Last term he had caught her talking to a boy from St Duncan's the night of a school dance, and got completely the wrong end of the stick. It had led to one of their most intense sexual encounters ever. Laura remembered the violence of his desire that night every time she was in the school art room, where it had taken place. Part of her had been terrified, part of her wanted the same again.

She was glad she didn't speak Italian and Giovanni, the guy she was dancing with, spoke no English. It meant she could just think her thoughts and not have to struggle to make conversation.

Though it wouldn't be a bad idea to learn Italian. She and Charlotte were already picking up a few words here and there. Knowing some French and Latin helped.

"Gio really likes you," Susie told her later that night.

Laura first thought she said "Zio" due to the background noise, and was momentarily confused. Zio Giorgio, Susie's uncle, didn't speak a word of English so she hadn't managed to converse with him at all.

"Your uncle?"

"God no, not Zio - Gio. Giovanni. He's pretty fit, don't you think?"

Laura agreed. At another time, in other circumstances, she might have been interested.

"I'm sure Zio Giorgio would be more than up for it as well, if you've decided to go for an even older man this time." Susie was teasing her, her eyes were laughing though she kept her face straight.

"Hardly. Imagine what your aunt would say."

"She'd be glad of the break I expect," Susie said. "Or the opportunity to have some fun of her own. She gets stifled playing the good Italian housewife, she's dying to take us all out and let her hair down."

2. Reunion

Susie arranged for her uncle's driver to take Laura to the airport to meet Mr Rydell the next afternoon. "I'm actually dying to come but I know you two are going to want your privacy. At least you can pull the screen shut if you can't wait until you get to the hotel."

Laura didn't understand what Susie meant until the driver opened the door for her, and she saw that there was a kind of screen between the front seat and the back seat that could be pulled across for privacy. Not that she could imagine using it for such a purpose in Susie's uncle's car, it was unthinkable. She also thought it might seem rude to the driver to pull it across, though perhaps he was used to it.

She was so nervous about seeing Mr Rydell again she was digging her nails into her fingers, trying to keep calm. She had built this encounter up in her mind so much that she was terrified something would go wrong.

Earlier that day Susie had dragged both Laura and Charlotte around the town for some clothes shopping. She had made Laura buy the most incredible lingerie - "seriously, he'll love it" - with a price tag over ten times higher than she had ever seen for underwear. It was made of pale blue silk and fragile lace and looked completely impractical.

"There's no way I can afford that!" Laura said.

"It's a present. Here," Susie handed over a credit card to the shop assistant, ignoring Laura's protests. "It's Zio Giorgio's, he and Zia Viola like to lavish gifts on me to annoy my parents. And don't worry, I'm sure I'll be repaying them in blood, sweat and tears when I eventually start working for the family firm."

"For the price, you're not getting much material are you?" Charlotte said, feeling the tiny scraps of silk and lace. "I can just imagine what Matron will say if you try and put that through the wash back at Francis Hall."

"It would disintegrate. You'll have to hand wash it," Susie told Laura. "That's if it survives the first night. The first hour, even. I expect he'll rip it off with his teeth."

Laura blushed and laughed at the same time. It felt strange but nice how her friends were preparing her for her meeting with Mr Rydell. She needed the moral support.

"Honestly, Susie, it's too expensive. I've already got some that I got with my Christmas money, I mean it's not quite like this, but it's okay."

"You can't spend the night at the Palazzo Calabria with a devastatingly handsome man, wearing Marks & Spencer's granny knickers. It's all wrong," Susie said. She cut Laura off with a wave of her hand and signed the credit card receipt, and handed her the miniature boutique bag they had been put into, carefully wrapped in tissue paper.

"I will pay you back," Laura said, though she had no clue how she would.

"No you won't, they're a gift. If you want to give me a gift back, I'm sure I'll need your help with something next term."

Laura and Charlotte exchanged a glance. They were both remembering Susie's legendary birthday party at school last year. The three of them had sneaked out their dormitory in the dead of night, met up with a load of St Duncan's boys in the school pavilion, and drunk beer and played poker until the janitor had nearly caught them red-handed.

It had been a very narrow escape. They had got away with it, but the memory still gave Laura a sensation of dread. She shuddered to think what further escapades Susie would be tempted to try during the next term. Either way, she knew they would all get roped in again to some risky scheme or other.

* * *

Seeing Mr Rydell again moved Laura's world. It may have only been a three week separation, but that was after having seen him nearly every day for over three months.

Across the airport Mr Rydell looked taller and older and she was momentarily terrified that he would reject her. But the expression on his face when he saw her assuaged all her fears. She was in his arms at once, she felt like crying with relief. She breathed in the familiarity of his smell, warm and masculine with a trace of shaving cream, burying her face against his chest. She could feel the hardness of his muscles through the dark wool of his jersey.

"God how I've missed you," he told her, stroking her hair, turning her face towards him and tilting it so he could kiss her.

She had been dreaming and longing for this. It was even better than she had visualised.

And now they had a whole week together. Laura was both elated at the thought of it, and already anxious at the prospect of it ending and having to part ways and start school again.

He laughed when he saw Susie's uncle's car. "I wasn't expecting a Rolls Royce with a chauffeur."

"They do seem to be pretty well off," Laura said, aware of what an understatement this was.

He was equally impressed by the hotel. Laura told him that Susie had arranged it all. "Apparently her uncle knows the owner so it's all free."

"I can't accept something like this from people I haven't even met," he said.

"They were actually happy to have you stay with them, but Susie thought we might like to be alone."

He pulled her against him as they entered the lift. "She was right. But I can't have her family pay for my stay."

"Talk to Susie about it. Maybe you can work something out." Laura knew it would be as hopeless for him to try and reject Susie's generosity as it had been for her.

The porter carried the luggage into the bedroom, Mr Rydell tipped him, and left. Laura looked around the room, fairly stunned. It looked like the honeymoon suite or something. There were huge vases of fresh flowers as well a bowl of fruit and a bottle of champagne in an ice bucket. She should have guessed Susie would go and do something lavish like this.

"Come here." It was a command, but one that Laura was only too happy to obey. She had been dying to be in his arms since she saw him, to be naked with him, for him to take her and make her his again.

He kissed her gently at first but she could feel the urgency and the desire within him for more. His lips were warm on hers, sensuous but also insistent. They had both had to wait too long for this.

Yet he took his time. He undressed her, leaving his own clothes on while he removed hers, until she stood there in nothing but the outrageously expensive and flimsy underwear that Susie had made her buy.

He drew in his breath. "Christ."

"Do you like it?" Now she was anxious. Was it too much?

"You look like a beautiful little courtesan, where the hell did you get that? No - don't tell me - I can guess." He didn't need to tell her how much he liked it in words, his actions spoke for him. He left it on her, putting his mouth over the thin lace covering her breast, teasing her through it. She felt the heat of his breath, the flick of his tongue.

He ran his fingers around the edge where it skimmed the curve of her rear, slipping them just underneath, making her shiver with anticipation.

"You can wear this for me every day, and nothing else," he said.

Laura smiled. "I might get arrested for public indecency."

"I don't plan to let you out of this room. Or out of my bed."

He was joking but there was a darkness in his eyes, a hunger. Half of him - and half of her - wanted her to be trapped here, ravished by him for an entire week.

His eyes were still drinking in her body. "You've lost weight."

"Not deliberately."

"Have you been ill?" He looked concerned.

She couldn't tell him that she had been lovesick. Nerves and lack of interest in other things had simply reduced her appetite. "Just a bug, and some stress thinking about schoolwork next term." She didn't like lying to him but it was sort of true. She was stressed thinking about the next term without him there.

"If you need my help you only have to ask. I know I won't be at Francis Hall next term, but I'm still there for you." He was trailing his fingers down her side and stomach, toying with her nipple through her bra. The silk was so thin that she could almost feel the ridges of his thumb. She thrilled at his touch.

He reached lower, towards her most intimate place, slipping his fingers underneath her clothing. She gave a jolt as he touched her flesh. "Are you ready for me?"

He could feel she was ready for him, she was wet and slick and longing for him to take her, but he wanted to hear her say it.

"Yes."

He carried her onto the bed and laid her down, still in the lingerie. He drew off his shirt and unbuckled his belt, and she shivered as she heard the clink of the metal. He was more than ready for her, springing rock hard as he rapidly pulled the rest of his clothes off.

Leaving the designer garments on her, he pushed the fabric across to one side, his fingers feeling inside her folds, the heat, the wetness.

Then he positioned himself and in one hard, direct thrust he pushed into into her, to full depth, and she gasped and cried out at the unexpectedness of it.

"Dressing up like that is playing with fire," he told her. "Wind me up like that and you will get what's coming to you."

They both had so much pent up energy for one another that it was the most vigorous lovemaking that Laura could remember. It also seemed to be endless. It was like he was driving into her for all the times he had missed in previous weeks.

"I love you, Christ how I love you." His face was strained with the exertion as he came, the extra hardness of him and the final sharp thrusts brought her over the edge as well. She writhed her hips against his, deeper and closer, sobbing as she also lost control.

He collapsed on top of her and she could hardly breathe under his weight, but she wanted the pressure. His presence. The sheer physicalness of him being with her.

His hair and skin, like hers, were damp with sweat. She was absolutely, utterly sated and yet as he lay on top of her after a few moments she started to get a feeling in her stomach that she wanted him again.

The way he was pressing down on her was stimulating her in some way. The way she couldn't move properly, the way she was trapped under the hard planes and muscle of his body. The smell of him, the fresh sweat. The warmth and proximity of his skin.

She squirmed around, needing more release, trying to manoeuvre her and at at first he thought he was crushing her and she was trying to get free. "Are you ok?"

"I'm fine, please stay there."

An amused light came into his eyes as he realised she was already turned on again. "Wasn't that enough for you?"

"Yes, but I just want it again already," she said, blushing at the admission.

"You'll have to give me some recovery time. In the meantime..." He slid down her body and parted her legs. He slid two fingers inside her, curling them around in her, stretching her gently. It was a very different sensation to him being inside her properly but it was having a strong effect on her.

With his other hand he spread her folds apart, using the heel of his palm to push her skin up, exposing her most sensitive spot. His mouth went over her and he sucked on it hard, just as his fingers twisted and tugged inside her.

Laura actually screamed as she came, the sensation was almost too much, so quickly. She didn't think she was nearly ready but he knew her body better than she did.

His mouth stayed over her as the waves ran through her, she was bucking against him. He was taking her through the pleasure to where it was almost painful but she still wasn't spent and he wouldn't stop.

She didn't know if it was seconds or minutes that the spasms ran through her but she was crying and dizzy before he finally released her. "Feel better now?"

"Yes." She buried her head in his chest, embarrassed at her own abandon.

Despite the exhaustion they couldn't sleep. It was still mid afternoon and the winter sun shone brilliantly into the room. But they lay there together for some time, side by side, at peace, covered by the thick white sheet.

Eventually he spoke. "Susie's aunt and uncle must be quite liberal if they're okay with all this. Or did she spin them one of her tales?"

"No, they know. Or her aunt does anyway, her uncle is really busy all the time. We only saw him at dinner."

"So her aunt knows about us?" he asked.

Laura tried to explain. "Yes, but she's sort of... Bohemian," she chose, not sure of a better term. "And they've got three grown up sons" - she felt him tense at this - "so I don't think they really notice or mind what Susie gets up to. It would probably be different if they were her parents."

"No wonder Susie is like she is," he said.

"Yes, she's just like her aunt. You'll love her aunt. She's incredibly beautiful, she used to dance and model and I'm sure she still could now, she looks so young."

"The sons live with them?" He couldn't completely conceal a flash of possessiveness in thinking that Laura had been spending her time with three rich Italian men.

Laura could hear the note of suspicion in his voice, and liked it. "Only Ferdinando, the youngest. He's incredibly good looking, he used to do some modelling but he doesn't really need to work. He drives a Ferrari, so fast I kept thinking we'd crash," she said, deliberately trying to wind him up.

It worked. She could feel him grow more tense beside her and sensed his mood darken.

"He's been showing us around the place. We went clubbing last night, it was amazing," she told him.

"Just you and Ferdinando?"

There was a dangerous note in his voice now. Laura didn't want to take it too far.

"His boyfriend is adorable too. Massimo. He's also a model."

Mr Rydell was silent for moment, and then he relaxed and laughed. "Thank god for Massimo," he said, partly under his breath.

3. An idyllic week

He was relentless with her in bed, they barely left the room for two days. Laura lost count of the times they made love, every position, every angle. She was exhausted, exhilarated, desperately in love with him.

Just one time he took her the other way. As with the last time in London he started as gently as possible and he went slowly. But this time he took her lying on her back, so he could look at her face while he entered her. She first thought he was about to do it normally until he went lower.

Once again she was a little scared but she trusted him. It was a different sensation to sexual pleasure: more of a yielding, of allowing him the use of her body. He grasped her hips and set the pace and the depth and she tried to relax and give him what he wanted from her.

It felt like he was going deeper into the core of her, stretching her, owning her.

"Am I hurting you?" he asked.

She told him no, but it wasn't entirely true.

"What does it feel like for you?"

"Like you're inside me, in the very centre of me."

She saw the desire darken his eyes and knew that she had given him the right answer. She couldn't really hide it from him though, when he thrust in fully each time, that there was some discomfort.

He moved his hand between her legs, swirling his finger around her most sensitive point. She gasped and arched towards his touch. But he left her core spot and circled around it instead, refusing to give her exactly what she craved.

"Not yet. I want to take this slowly with you," he told her.

Whenever his finger brushed over her in the exact place she felt a throb which turned any discomfort to pleasure. Then he would move it around her for a while, continuing to push in and out of her. He wanted to link any pain she felt with pleasure.

He wanted her submission, to submit to him because she desired him so much.

"Tell me what it's like when I'm inside you like this," he asked her.

She wasn't sure what to say or what he wanted to hear. "It's sort of heavy, and there's nothing else in the world but you."

"And what do you want from me?"

"More of you." It was barely a whisper but it conveyed all he needed to know. She was entirely his.

He finally allowed her more stimulation where she needed it, watching her face as he did so and the conflicted emotions that crossed it. Confusion, fear, desire.

She was so tight around him, skin on skin. He was so hard and swollen now he could barely hold back, so he increased the pace. At first it hurt and she bit her lip and shifted but with his other hand he held her still and thrust faster and faster.

Now her pressed on her button directly, firmly, with the flat of his thumb. She bucked against him, whimpering. With the sensations growing there she barely noticed any pain or discomfort, she just desperately needed release.

He was able to go harder and deeper and her body was reaching towards him, finally wanting the depth, embracing it.

Laura closed her eyes and let it take her over. She was overwhelmed, physically and emotionally. She could hear him saying things to her, how much he loved her, how much he desired her, how beautiful she was, but it felt like he was far away.

She stopped thinking, she couldn't speak, she could only feel. When it was finally over, when the waves had finished passing through, she wanted oblivion. She felt disconnected from him. The world seemed tilted, as though she was lying on a downwards gradient.

He could sense something was wrong. "Was that too much?" He was worried now, his hair falling over his forehead, looking at her with concern. "I didn't want to hurt you."

But he had wanted to, in a strange, dark way and they both knew it. Yet he hadn't hurt her. It was as though in reaching for her, in trying to take her and own her wholly, she only slipped further away.

Laura looked at him. His face, its flawless angles, which she loved. The set of his eyes and their dark grey colour. The texture of his skin, shadowed with stubble from not shaving that day.

She felt an overwhelming love for him. She rejoiced in being with him, she felt luckier than anything to be the one he had chosen. For him to feel the same way about her that she did about him.

Yet there was something else. A flash of something that she buried deep down within herself.

She smiled at him, and let him kiss her and hold her, and the world gently tipped back to where it was supposed to be.

* * *

They were awoken early the second morning by a loud knocking at the door. It was Susie.

"It's time you two stopped hiding away. Zia Viola wants you to come to dinner, she's dying to meet you," she said.

"What are you doing up so early? It's barely dawn," Laura said. The curtains were only half drawn and she could see the lightening sky beyond them.

"I've been up all night, we went to a party."

Unlike most people staying up all night, Susie still looked fresh and full of energy. She was wearing a tight black dress with an asymmetric neckline and the smoky aroma of nightclubs clung to her.

Laura was wrapped in a sheet, her hair tousled.

Susie gave a sly grin. "Imagine if Mrs Grayson could see you both now. Mr Rydell without his jacket and tie, in bed with a Michaelmas girl."

The image of their headmistress appearing at the door was simultaneously so absurd and so alarming that Laura felt a lurch. "Don't tempt fate. Where's Charlotte?"

Susie's grin became wider. "Downstairs in the lobby with Gio. He needed consoling after your cruel rejection the other night."

"Gio?" Mr Rydell's tone held everything it needed to.

"Nothing to fear. He's just a playboy, goes after any foreign girl in town," Susie said to reassure him. Laura suspected it would not but she wanted to change the subject.

"What are you both doing today?" For her own part she was reluctant to leave the bubble of just her and Mr Rydell, but they couldn't be so rude as to refuse a dinner invitation. After all she was supposed to be their guest.

"I'm going back to shower and sleep, then we'll probably get up around midday and go sightseeing. That way we can get some photos, so Charlotte can pretend to her father that she spent the whole trip studying history and culture."

"We should probably do the same," Laura said.

She loved the idea of being able to walk around openly with Mr Rydell, something they could hardly do back home. To actually be in public as a couple. Somewhere that no one knew them and where they were safe to act as they liked.

"It will give me a chance to brush up on my rusty Italian," he said.

"You speak Italian?" Susie hadn't known this.

"Barely."

"I'll have to warn Aunt Viola, in case she says anything outrageous that's not intended for your ears," Susie said. "Or maybe I won't, it might be more fun if she says something compromising and discovers your ability that way."

* * *

After a day of sightseeing and given the limited amount she had slept over the past few days, Laura felt exhausted. Susie had dropped off a dress for her to wear that night, black and slinky, as Laura's clothes were still at Susie's family's villa.

Miraculously the expensive, fragile lingerie had survived, and she had carefully washed and dried it in the hotel room. She slipped it on again now, getting ready to put her dress on.

"You can't wear that. I'll be distracted all evening by the thought of it under your clothes."

She loved how much he wanted her.

"Take me now then." At least he could get it out of his system.

"I would love to, more than anything, but we don't have time."

In response Laura came over to him, put his hands on her body, and pressed herself against him. "So we'll be late."

She knew that he couldn't resist her if she teased him like this, and she loved the sense of power it gave her over him. On so many other levels there was still this imbalance between them. Mr Rydell was older, far more experienced, independent of school and parents and all the things that constrained her own freedom. He had seen far more of the world than she had.

Yet she could seduce him any time she wanted. No matter how reserved, determined or in control he tried to be, it was the one battle she could always win. And it gave her confidence that she had something that he wanted so badly.

Because what else could he see in her? She suffered from so much self doubt about this. The others had tried to reassure her about her looks, about her personality, about being interesting but it didn't help. She feared that she was too young, too unworldly and unremarkable, to hold his regard indefinitely.

He wouldn't just take his own pleasures from her, though. He insisted that she climaxed with him every time, refusing to leave her unsatisfied. Now he bent her over the bed, pulling the fabric to the side once again. Pushing inside her gently this time. The perfect fit.

Reaching around her. Knowing exactly how to play her body: what would swell and bud under his touch. How he could bring her down with him as well to hopeless, helpless lust.

They managed it in minutes, though Laura would have liked to have gone straight to bed with him afterwards. Neither of them had any desire to leave the room but nonetheless they did so, Susie's uncle's driver picking them up from the lobby.

Mr Rydell had the same reaction that Laura and Charlotte had had to the villa gates.

"I told you they were loaded," Laura said. "Not that they chose those gates, Susie says they were some mafia lord's."

Zia Viola was wearing a gold silk sheath that clung to her curves and made her look like Susie's older sister. She was exceptionally charming, showing genuine delight in meeting Mr Rydell and calling him Signor. She also referred to him as "*fidanzato*" which Susie translated as "fiancé".

"I know you guys aren't engaged, and god forbid you elope to Sicily or something idiotic like that, but it's a more elegant word than boyfriend. Actually it gets used for both anyway," Susie explained.

Mr Rydell found it amusing, and started referring to Laura as "*mia fidanzata*". His Italian was more impressive than he had led them to believe: although he was far from fluent, he could manage enough to converse with both Zia Viola and Zio Giorgio.

Dinner was a huge success. Susie's uncle monopolised the new guest, mainly because he was the only person he could converse with other than his family. Susie chattered in rapid Italian with her aunt and cousin, and Laura and Charlotte were finally able to have something of their own conversation.

"I'm still trying to get used to seeing you two together," Charlotte said. "Openly I mean. Don't you sometimes get freaked out that Mrs Grayson or someone will suddenly appear?"

Laura admitted that she did. "Being this far away helps though.

"He really is amazing, isn't he? Look at him talking away to Uncle Giorgio. I had no idea how we were all going to manage to communicate."

Laura looked at him across the table. She felt lost again and she couldn't put her finger on why. "Do they know about us? I mean that he was one of our teachers."

Charlotte wasn't sure. "If they do I don't think they'd care. Everything seems to be very different with them. I don't know if it's being Italian or being so rich, to be honest."

Everything was beautiful there: the table setting, the lighting, the food. The clothes people wore. It felt strangely like a pageant.

"I meant to ask you about what happened with you and Gio," Laura said. "Do you like him?"

"He's very good looking, it was just a bit of fun though. It didn't go anywhere."

"What about Julian?"

Charlotte looked uncomfortable. "I don't know. I really like him, of course, but it's not like we're going to end up together, is it? Once he leaves St Duncan's he'll be surrounded by other girls. It's not like you and Mr Rydell. You two seem destined."

This gave Laura a happy lurch in her stomach. "Really?"

"There's something about the pair of you. When they were calling you his fiancée or whatever it was in Italian, it just seemed normal. Obvious."

Laura watched him across the table as he took his glass, laughing at something Susie's uncle had told him. He clearly knew Italian well enough to joke in it. She made a mental note to try and learn it better herself. From the little that she and Charlotte had picked up so far it seemed easier than German or French.

4. A day out

Zia Viola insisted that Susie, Charlotte and Laura come shopping with her the next morning. Her husband had already arranged to take Laura's *fidanzato* on a tour somewhere, she told them via Susie, so they would have plenty of time to spend in the boutiques of Reggio.

"If you thought my shopping was lavish wait until you see what my aunt is like," Susie told them. They had the use of the driver as Zio Giorgio was using his own car.

Stepping into the car as the driver held the doors open for them, Laura wondered how long it took to become accustomed to this kind of luxury. Everything was made comfortable and convenient for them at every step. Zia Viola didn't even have to worry about carrying her own shopping bags as they were quickly and discreetly picked up by the driver as they left each store.

Yet she never seemed arrogant or entitled, it was just that she simply accepted these things would be done. Laura found her strangely childlike as much as she was one of the most beautiful and sophisticated women she had ever met. Zia Viola was a happy person. Even if she had been poor, Laura suspected, she would have been just the same.

Zia Viola also insisted on buying them presents. "She says that she's had three sons for long enough, finally she has three daughters for the day and she plans to make the most of it," Susie told them.

Laura knew her parents would never let her accept expensive gifts from Susie's relatives so it made her feel extremely awkward. She could sense that Charlotte felt the same.

"This is a gift for her, not you," Susie explained when her aunt was out of earshot. "Just indulge her. She's the one who's getting the most enjoyment out of this. Be glad it's not Milan or Rome or things would be even more insane."

So they both tried to hide their discomfort and be as gracious as possible, while steering Zia Viola to items that didn't seem absurdly expensive. Laura tried to suggest she liked a scarf instead of a dress, imagining that it must be much cheaper.

"She'll only buy you both," Susie said. "So you may as well be honest about what you like."

Both Laura and Charlotte ended up with little black dresses. The deceptively simple look of Laura's dress belied its vast price tag. She knew that there were already a couple of thousand lira to the pound but that still couldn't accommodate the endless zeros.

Charlotte was thrilled with her dress. "My father would go mad if he saw me wearing anything like this. It's so short!"

"That's because you're so tall," Susie said.

"One of you will have to take it back in your luggage for me. I can't risk my parents finding it," Charlotte told them.

Laura faced a similar dilemma with her designer underwear. At least when folded a black dress looked pretty much like any other black dress. She offered to hide Charlotte's for her.

They had lunch at a pizzeria which was Susie's choice, suspecting that her friends could do with a break from the more exclusive end of town. They never had to worry about parking thanks to the driver, who dropped them off wherever needed even if it meant stopping in mid-traffic. Laura found the honking of car horns whenever this happened very embarrassing.

"They're honking at you and Charlotte, they couldn't care less about the car," Susie told them.

Pizza at least seemed like a slice of normality. Even if it was by far the best pizza Laura had ever eaten. A thin, crispy crust that had bubbled in the hot oven, with fresh Mozzarella melted on top of the sweet tomato paste, scattered with olives and fresh herbs that had gone crispy, releasing their aromatic oils into the topping. All the food they seemed to get in Italy was amazing.

She suppressed a shudder at the thought of school food back at Francis Hall. She had chosen to go vegetarian last term to get out of eating liver and some of the other horrendous slop served up by the dinner ladies. Returning to alternating days of grated cheese and boiled eggs after the cuisine of Calabria was going to be tough.

To be polite but also because she was interested, Laura tried holding a conversation with Zia Viola via Susie. Charlotte was busy being distracted by one of the waiters who had been eyeing her up since they arrived. She was so blonde and statuesque, she turned heads everywhere.

After a while Laura got the hang of it and it didn't seem to matter having Susie as an interlocutor. From time to time Laura figured out a few things Zia Viola was saying before Susie translated them. They mainly talked of school: how theirs compared to the strict Catholic convent that Zia Viola had been sent to - "confined to", as Susie translated - in her youth, and how she had circumvented the rules and driven the nuns to despair.

Many of Zia Viola's anecdotes, possibly embellished by Susie, were quite outrageous. Laura had no way of knowing how much was true and how much was exaggerated, but given the flashing laughter in Zia Viola's dark eyes and what they all knew of Susie's own behaviour at Francis Hall, she was inclined to believe most of it.

They had decided it would be wise to get some more photos that afternoon to prove they had been visiting historic sites. Zia Viola said something in Italian and Susie nodded. "We should go and see the bronzes, they're the most famous thing here."

"My father is bound to ask about them then," Charlotte said.

Laura had already read about the statues in her guidebook. The Riace bronzes were life size statues of Greek warriors, found in the sea a few years ago. They were the pride of the city and there were endless photos and postcards of them all over the place.

Zia Viola declined to accompany to them to the archaeological museum. "My aunt has a party tonight and wants to relax at home first," Susie explained. "She's also seen them a million times."

There was no need to drive as the museum was in the heart of the town. It was a huge, imposing structure, elegant on the outside with airy galleries within. Large windows provided a lot of natural light, displaying its many statues to their best advantage.

"It rather puts Welchester Museum in the shade, doesn't it?" Charlotte remarked, referring to a Roman museum near Francis Hall, where school trips were often taken. "And I don't mean just the relics." A dark-eyed museum tour guide had been sending her some smouldering looks.

"You're turning into a nympho," Laura said.

Charlotte sighed. "I don't know how I'm going ever find pasty British boys attractive ever again. Italy has ruined me for men."

Susie was laughing. "They're not all that great. You must have a thing for Latin lovers or something."

"Like Mr Tyrrell?" Laura said and couldn't stop laughing as well. Their Latin teacher was considered a sweet man but very old and dry. "You were sucking up to him last term, if you remember Charlotte. Was there something behind that you weren't telling us?"

In the dark metal flesh the Riace bronzes were far more imposing than she could have imagined. They were also far more life-like. Something about the way their muscles were moulded, by their ancient sculptor, was oddly realistic.

Obviously you couldn't touch them but Laura would liked to have felt them under her hands. She had sculpted her first human figurine from clay the previous term and it had become much easier once she had felt the muscles and planes of Mr Rydell's torso.

The statues drew her and she found herself longing for him again. She was still in a surreal state of joy being with him in Italy. It was like an entirely different life.

* * *

Mr Rydell met them later in the town and Laura's heart leapt when she saw him approaching. He was so tall and commanding. She still couldn't believe as he walked towards her that he was hers. That she was with this man.

Then as he kissed her in greeting and put his arm around her she felt strangely shy and also cut off from Susie and Charlotte, who were doubtless nudging themselves and grinning.

There was still a barrier between her friends and him. They still viewed him as Mr Rydell, teacher, whereas Laura was in a kind of no man's land. He treated her as his equal yet he still very much took the lead.

"Are we dining together?" he asked and Susie put the question to her aunt.

"As you like" was the reply in Italian.

"You should go somewhere just the two of you," Susie said. "Make the most of your time here."

Laura could tell that this was what Mr Rydell wanted to do, but while she longed to be alone with him she also felt left out of the fun that Charlotte and and Susie would be having. She briefly imagined what it would be like if they all had their boyfriends there. Would the three men get on together or would it be awkward?

She had the impression that Darius would be at ease in any company. He shared that quality with Susie: they were both far too worldly for their years. They stood apart. Julian was also more of a man than a schoolboy, he was rugby captain after all. Yet Laura thought it probably wouldn't sit as well with him as with Darius. He was still in that school sphere, as she, Charlotte and Margery were.

Susie and her aunt gave them some recommendations and they parted ways, with Laura and Mr Rydell going back to his hotel. Laura still thought of it as his even though the room was booked for both of them.

It was the first time they had been out for dinner together since London, she realised. That was months ago. Compared to back in England Laura got constant looks and attention from Italian men. It would have been flattering but she was more fearful that he would think she was encouraging it.

She could tell he was tense though he didn't say anything. He didn't criticise her top which was lower cut than she had intended, though she knew he was aware of other men staring at her there.

She was very glad she hadn't risked wearing the dress Susie had bought her as it was even tighter and sexier.

"You practically need a bodyguard here," he remarked. He wasn't entirely joking.

Once they were seated it was easier as other diners around them were already in couples and if any men were glancing at her, they were doing so far more discreetly. Laura wasn't used to this kind of attention. In England she felt unremarkable, just one of the crowd. Here she stood out because she was blonde and clearly a foreigner. Even though there were spectacularly beautiful Italian women all over the place. The average person here was so much more attractive and glamorous than back home.

Over dinner she was able to relax and just enjoy being with him. She still marvelled how easy it was to talk to him, how much they had in common despite their vastly different life experiences. She knew he was officially her boyfriend but she didn't yet feel she could take that for granted.

At one point he took her hand and looked into her eyes. "You are the most beautiful girl in the room." His thumb caressed her palm and she was in raptures for a moment, not knowing how to respond. So she just gazed back at him.

She could see in his eyes how much he loved her and desired her but also that he was struggling with it. She wasn't sure why and she felt unable to ask.

5. Night of passion

"Finally mine."

Back at the hotel Mr Rydell stripped her clothes off her as soon as they were in the room.

"I've been wanting you all night, I thought I would go mad in that restaurant."

Laura gloried in his urgency, in his overpowering need for her. He didn't remove any of his own clothes, perhaps deliberately he kept them on. She wasn't sure but it was an interesting change. She was fully naked and he was fully clothed.

She felt the roughness of fabric against her skin. She tried to reach under his shirt to touch him, wanting to feel his skin and the hard angles of his muscle. But he stopped her, pushing her hands away.

"Tonight you are mine. I want to remind you what that means."

He wanted to make it all about her. She was the object of his desire: he wanted her helpless under his touch, exposed to him, defenceless.

His hands went everywhere over her body, running down her sides in the curve of her waist, brushing over her stomach. Gently over her breasts then with increasing firmness, moulding their roundness into his grasp.

His hands parted her thighs, pushing them apart and opening her to him. For a few moments he gazed over her body and suddenly she felt self-conscious and tried to close her legs but he held them firmly.

Then he was between them, his mouth covering her. She felt him hot and warm over her. His tongue went firmly over her most sensitive area. She squirmed against him as he pressed her down into the bed, gripping her thighs and limiting her movement.

Often he made her wait for release but tonight he wanted to prove he could conquer her in minutes.

He slipped two fingers inside her and somehow his attentions to the front of her made her extra sensitive inside. The combination of feeling his mouth on her, pressing and tonguing her as hard as he could, and the firmness of his fingers inside her, probing and curling was too much.

She was nothing but a ball of sensation between her legs, tightly wound, throbbing. She clutched his hair not knowing if she wanted him to lessen or increase the pressure, or whether she just wanted to touch him.

The silence of the room magnified the sound of her own breathing but she couldn't control it. She bit her lip to try and quieten herself but he had started a rhythm with his hands and mouth and it was making her gasp.

She was worried people in the next room would hear. She tried covering her own face with her hands to try and muffle herself.

And he continued, relentless. Until she was spasming in waves underneath him.

"Oh god I want you." She was crying out, losing herself. Clutching the sheets in her hands, writhing against him. It went on and on, and even as she became too over sensitised he continued.

Just as the feelings abated and it was nearly uncomfortable she felt them bubble up inside her again. It had never happened like this.

He kept going, constant in his attentions and pressure, and she came once more, almost immediately after the first time.

Her eyes were closed and she felt tears at the corners though she didn't think she had been crying.

Then he drew himself up over her and brushed the hair from the side of her face. His expression showed tenderness rather than the hunger she expected. He had seemed almost angry when they started but now she saw nothing but love there. In a strange way it unsettled her more than if he had been wild with passion.

"There won't ever be anyone else for you but me, Laura. I want you forever."

His words were possessive. For a moment she wondered if he had meant to say "anyone else but you" but looking at his face, she understood he had said what he intended.

She wanted to give him the release he had given her, and she shifted so she could ease him inside her. They rocked together, drowning in one another, wishing it could last forever.

She was his, he never needed to doubt it. She told him this and she could feel it bringing him closer. "Only you, always you."

His orgasm was powerful, almost hurting her with the strength of his final thrusts. He grasped her hips and ground into her as deep as he could be. They were a single flesh.

He stayed inside her for some time before finally easing off her and nestling her to his chest, side by side. He fell asleep before she did and she lay there, thinking and wondering. How things might have been if she had never met him. How bleak life would be without him.

If days and nights were jewels this one would have been a ruby. Deep red with a dark fire flickering within. But Laura wasn't sure if she did, or should, fear that dark flame.

* * *

Laura awoke first shortly after daybreak and looked at him, still sleeping. She remembered the first time she had awoken in his bed, in his lodgings at Francis Hall the morning after he had taken her virginity. How awkward she had felt then, how panicked that she had disappointed him and that he wouldn't want her again.

Now she was more confident in what she could do to his body, and the effect her body had on him. She still had moments of doubt that she might not be the best lover he had ever had but she buried these deep within her. For her part, she could not imagine it being better with anyone else than it was with him.

She loved him so much. He was everything to her.

They showered together and made love again. Had breakfast in their room so they could lie in bed as long as possible.

Outside the sun was dazzlingly bright, the kind of stark brilliance only seen in winter. It was their last day in Italy before flying home on the next morning. Her last day with him.

The others were going to visit Mount Etna that day, across the sea in Sicily. It was over three hours drive so they had left early in the morning. Laura and Mr Rydell had been invited but had chosen to stay in Reggio.

Laura was a little bit torn over not seeing the volcano but Susie assured her there would be future opportunities. "Aunt Viola will insist on you all visiting again. She already adores you and she's fascinated by your forbidden romance."

They were all meeting up later that evening anyway for a final meal. Susie's aunt had wanted to throw them a party but Susie dissuaded her. "Just us all together will be more fun." She and Charlotte had gone out on the town again the previous evening, going to a party with some of Ferdinando's friends.

* * *

They spent most of the day on the seafront. You could stroll all the way past the ruins of Roman baths, looking out over the Strait of Messina towards Sicily and snow-capped Mount Etna. The *lungomare* promenade milled with people: singles, couples and families pushing prams past the palm trees and landscaped gardens the bordered the beach. Laura loved being part of it.

"Susie says you can see a mirage here in summer," she said.

"We'll come back in summer then. We can travel around Italy if you like," Mr Rydell suggested.

It was a lovely dream. They had nearly nine weeks summer holiday in July and August. Laura could easily manage it around her family's annual fortnight in France. She would probably have to use Susie as cover again.

"It's a pity we don't have longer this time, I could have taken you skiing," he said.

Laura had never skied before. "Is it hard to learn?"

"Not very. But it's enjoyable even if you're a beginner."

She couldn't resist the innuendo. "Like other things?"

Mr Rydell laughed. "Like other things. But you're hardly a beginner any more."

"Thanks to your expert tuition." She reached up to him and he kissed her, his lips firm but tender on hers. She was drowning in joy and desire. It was ecstatic being able to kiss him openly like this. No one to bother them or stop them or report them.

He broke off, his hands still twined in her hair, tilting her face towards him. "It helps to have an apt and willing pupil."

* * *

Charlotte had called Mr Rydell "Sir" at dinner without even realising until the others laughed at her. They were all so used to it as an appellation for male teachers that it just slipped out.

He reminded Laura of this as they went back to the hotel. "I seem you remember you calling me by that title on previous occasions. How come you don't do so any more?"

"I can if you like."

"I would like it, in the appropriate circumstances."

She shivered, wondering what he would want from her that night. It would be their last time for weeks and they both wanted it to be memorable. It had to last them until half term.

As they entered the room she turned to him. "Do you have some homework for me, Sir?"

"I think you could use a detention."

"What am I being punished for?"

He grinned. "Failure to do your German teacher enough."

"I think I need some more German oral practice." She knelt before him and undid his zip. He sprang out as she reached inside, already rock hard. She put her mouth over him, letting her hair fall over her face. She knew he liked this and that he would brush it back for her.

He groaned as she enclosed him, using her hands and her tongue to stimulate him as much as possible. She tried to take her lead from his reactions to different things she tried. Flicking the tip of her tongue around him, cupping him, moving her hands and head in the same rhythm. She wanted to have the same effect on him as he did on her for this.

He put his hands on her shoulders and she could hear how ragged his breathing was becoming. Although he usually took the initiative he seemed to love it when she did.

He let her continue for a while but he didn't want to finish that way. As she could feel him getting closer, growing even harder and more swollen in her mouth, he pulled her up. "I think your discipline is going to require a few hard strokes."

"Of the cane?"

He laughed. "I had something else in mind."

They were both still fully clothed and he took her clothes off as she removed his. Laura loved being able to do this, it made him feel like hers to be able to unbutton his shirt and pull it off him. His chest and muscles underneath were all hers to enjoy.

He felt between her legs. She was wet and swollen for him, longing for him to touch her more intimately. "I don't think you're supposed to be enjoying this so much. This might require extra correction."

"How much?"

"I think at least twenty strokes, rather than ten."

He pushed her down onto the bed on her stomach and at first she wasn't sure if he was going to actually spank her, but he pushed her legs apart with his knees and thrust straight into her without warning causing her to cry out.

Hard and unyielding he drove into her exactly twenty times, counting after each five.

Then just as suddenly he withdrew from her and she realised the real punishment was him stopping. "You can't do that!"

"You haven't been punished enough? You need more?"

"Much more." She was pleading with him.

He was enjoying her need for him. "Beg me then."

"Please."

"Please what?"

Her body was on fire, she needed him back inside her. "Please fuck me."

"Sir" he reminded her.

"Please fuck me, Sir."

And he did. She craved him, she felt like she would go out of her mind if he didn't keep driving into her, on and on. It was the closeness of him, the sense of fullness. The sensation for her own jangled nerves, both soothed and stimulated by him.

She would probably be sore tomorrow but right now she didn't care. Thankfully he had the stamina to meet her desire and he pounded her for as long as she needed. When she came it took her by surprise. He usually reached around and played with her, touched her in specific places to bring her over the edge. Or she would angle herself and press against him if she was face to face with him.

This time she was face down on the bed. She couldn't see him, she could only hear him. She had lost track of time, there was only her body and the feeling of him and what he was doing to her.

Then suddenly there were extra sharp feelings bubbling up inside her and she realised she was reaching the peak. She cried out but he just kept up his rhythm which prolonged it for her, it felt as though it would never end. She didn't even know or feel if he had come, and in the moment she didn't even care.

He lay beside her. "Better now?"

She buried her face in the pillow, suddenly self-conscious. "More than better. I wish you could know how good it is for me."

"It was pretty clear."

Laura rolled around to look at him. She put her hand on his face, tracing its angles. "I wish I could make you feel that way."

"You do. Trust me," he told her.

"Really?" She wanted confirmation.

He looked serious for a moment. "You have no idea, do you? How incredibly hot it is to have a girl like you call me Sir, and then kneel down like that."

"You did ask me to," she said.

"I know. But I probably shouldn't have."

She didn't understand why. He tried to explain.

"I shouldn't be getting off on the fact that you're so much younger than me, that you were my pupil. It makes me feel manipulative."

Laura took his hand and put it on her breast, closing his fingers around her flesh. "I like being manipulated."

"I love you regardless of the circumstances in which we met. I don't want you to ever get confused about that. It's not because you're younger than me," he said.

Did it matter if they both got an extra kick out of it? She didn't need him to be so much older than her, but she often enjoyed the fact that he was. His concerns were confusing her so she went to kiss him to distract him from the issue, and they lay together and fell asleep in one another's arms.

6. Spring term

From the freedom and luxuries of Southern Italy, returning to the regimented reality of school was an uncomfortable adjustment. Everything at Francis Hall seemed so much darker.

It was the darkest term: still buried in winter the days were short and snow was forecast. Their uniforms seemed dark. The classrooms seemed dim and shadowy. Chill draughts blew through the corridors. Even the red brick of the building looked dull and severe, with no summer sun to soften it and make it glow. It even smelt cold, the usual dust and wood and brick taking on a strange cold aroma.

"It's like living in a Victorian prison," Charlotte complained as she tried to warm her hands on a radiator to find it stone cold.

Most of all there was a dark emptiness where Mr Rydell had been. Laura could no longer look forward to his classes, their illicit meetings, even glimpses of him at lunch or in assembly where their eyes would meet and her stomach would turn over. She had never got used to the thrill of being with him.

The openness in Italy had been a wonderful thing but it was a different world. Here, she was back to secrecy, to the terrible, dangerous joy and knowledge of whom she loved and who loved her.

Except he wasn't there. There was only the hope of his letters, the occasional phone call from the payphone at Michaelmas house, which they would have to carefully coordinate at a time when they wouldn't be overheard. It didn't help that Laura's housemistress, Grace Grant, had guessed what was going on and would doubtless be keeping a sharp eye on her.

It wasn't enough. Even knowing that she would see him at half term wasn't enough. She had wanted to see him at the first exeat, in a few weeks' time, but he would be overseas.

"I think I'm actually getting frostbite."

Susie was shivering as they lined up outside the chapel for assembly on the first morning. She was also hoping to avoid the Head of English, Mr Peters, and his lecherous attentions. It had amused her last term but she was done with it now. Susie needed to find herself some new amusements. She rubbed her fingers, trying to get some warmth into them.

"You could wear gloves," Laura suggested.

"I hate the feel of that scratchy wool around my fingers." The gloves that were part of the Francis Hall uniform were thick, woollen garments in the ubiquitous school colour, maroon.

They filed in and took their places on the hard wooden benches. It was freezing inside the chapel as well. Any heat generated by the ancient radiators just wafted up to the vaulted ceiling leaving the congregation in a chilly draught below.

Laura found her eyes automatically going to where the staff sat near the altar end, searching for the face that had been there every morning last term, then remembering he was no longer there.

A hymn was sung, voices sounding thinner and reedier and the organ wheezy on this first day of term. A prayer was said, Laura using the time to think of other things, and the usual notices were given out by Mrs Grayson, the headmistress of Francis Hall. She looked the same as ever: stern, elegant and commanding.

The announcements included introducing new staff which was rather unusual in Spring term. Some woman called Elisabeth Beinhof, apparently an old university friend of the headmistress, would be taking them for German after the departure of Mr Rydell. Mrs Grayson invited her to say a few words.

Frau Beinhof was a tall, slender woman with light grey hair. She had a very fine bone structure and was quite beautiful, Laura thought. She must have been exceptionally lovely in her younger days. Like their headmistress, Frau Beinhof also looked fiercely intelligent. But fortunately not the dour, humourless kind of intellect that you sometimes got in teachers. She seemed interesting and like someone who enjoyed teaching and enjoyed her subject.

So far, so good. Deprived of the attraction of Mr Rydell they were going to need something to motivate their German studies this term.

The news that he had left sent a ripple of disappointment and curiosity around the rows of girls. Very few people, except Laura and her friends and a couple of others, had any idea he was leaving nor why.

"Was he sacked?"

"Maybe he had an illness in the family."

"Perhaps he left to get married?"

Charlotte heard this last one and gave Laura a sharp nudge, which caused her to half choke and half cough and then have to bury her head in her hymnbook. The beady eye of their sworn enemy, Teresa Hubert, saw everything.

Fortunately no one else appeared to notice. Mrs Grayson continued her announcements.

"Now I have some good news for you all. As you know, since the departure of Mr Carlisle last summer we have been without a coordinator for the Duke of Edinburgh award programme. I'm glad to say that our new geography teacher Mr Hollier, who replaces Mrs Ayers while she is on a leave of absence due to illness, will be stepping in."

Everyone knew Mrs Ayers had essentially gone insane, violently attacking Susie in the courtyard one day after months of mutual hatred between the pair. It had been officially described as a "nervous breakdown".

"This means that all fourth, fifth and lower sixth form girls will be doing the Bronze award" - there was a suppressed groan at this - "with the Lower School undertaking orienteering practice on Saturday afternoons and the lower sixth on Wednesdays."

There was some fairly vicious muttering going on now. No one wanted to have their precious free time wrested away, and Saturday afternoons were treasured for this. Girls that didn't play on sports teams essentially got a free half day.

"I am sure you'll all greatly enjoy this opportunity," Mrs Grayson told them. Her tone suggested that this was an instruction, not a prediction. "As you will be aware, completion of the award looks very favourable on your university applications. It will add an extra string to your bow. And now I'd like to introduce Mr Hollier, who will say a few words."

This turned the tide of interest in the headmistress's favour. Mr Hollier was tall and athletic looking, probably in his mid twenties. He didn't have the devastating looks of Mr Rydell but he was undeniably good looking in a wholesome, smiling way.

Laura remembered how Mr Rydell hadn't smiled a single time during the entire assembly of his introduction. It had made him seem more remote and increased his attractiveness, for her anyway. Mr Hollier, who smiled from the outset, looked much more approachable.

"Wish we were doing Geography now," someone muttered behind them.

"I wouldn't mind getting lost in the woods with him."

Mr Hollier received far more attention and analysis than Frau Beinhof had, but that was always the way with male teachers. Starved of access to boys, any male member of staff was fair game for romantic fantasy. It was pretty rare that such fantasy became reality, as it had done for Laura. But it was something to distract themselves with.

Charlotte and Margery, their fourth dorm mate who hadn't come to Italy with them, were discussing the new geography teacher as they walked from assembly to their first class. "I thought he looked a bit like Gilbert Blythe, you know, in Anne of Green Gables," Charlotte was saying.

"He looked nothing like him at all. He didn't even have the same hair."

"Well you know what I mean. But if they make me give up hockey to go orienteering I'll murder him, no matter how good looking he is." Charlotte was already concerned about what the new orienteering practice would mean for her. She was the only girl in the Lower School to have been selected for the First Eleven hockey team. Matches would now clash with this stupid Duke of Edinburgh thing, and she was determined to get some kind of exemption. Surely playing sport for the school was more important?

"I should think you'll be fine," Laura told her. "Your hockey is an ample 'string to your bow' or whatever Mrs Grayson said."

"I hope so, I really do. Otherwise Susie is going to have to try and get rid of him for me." Susie's Machiavellian machinations had helped tip Mrs Ayers over the edge the previous term.

Susie grinned. "He looks a bit robust for that strategy. Still, if you really want him gone I'm sure we can arrange something. Perhaps Laura could work her magic and deliberately get caught in flagrante?"

"Then they'd both be expelled," Margery said. "Just go and ask Miss Partridge about the orienteering thing, I'm sure she can sort it out for you. They probably just forgot that the time would clash for you." Miss Partridge was the schools sports coach and responsible for selecting the hockey team.

German and Geography, held at the same time because pupils only took one or other of the subjects, were the first classes that day. Susie went off to the Geography classrooms and the other three headed towards the languages block.

"It's an awful lot of change for the Spring term," Charlotte said. "Last term was pretty eventful, I suppose."

The ground was frozen and the grass was frost-white and crunched beneath their feet as they took the short cut around the chapel. "I don't know why they call it Spring term," Margery said. "It should be Winter term."

"Apparently this kills grass. Walking on it while it's frozen," Laura said.

"I'm sure it will grow back. If we're in for a bitter winter they can hardly close the hockey pitches all term." Charlotte hoped they wouldn't anyway.

Margery hoped for the exact opposite but kept quiet.

7. Lessons begin

Frau Beinhof had a novel approach to teaching her classes. She repeated everything in both languages: first English, then German. "I know that you are all relatively new to German and will doubtless understand very little of what I am saying at first," she told them, repeating the words in her native language. "But over time it will help accustom your ears to the sounds and rhythm of German, and I hope that some of it may sink in."

It made lessons more interesting, anyway. After a while Laura did find that she could pick out certain words and phrases. Beyond that it was simply nice to listen to as Frau Beinhof had a good speaking voice and managed to make German sound more musical and less guttural.

Frau Beinhof was also pleased with their general grasp of German after just one term studying it. This was partly credit to Mr Rydell's teaching, but more so to the zeal with which girls had studied German hoping to win his favour.

Teresa Hubert had been giving Laura scowls and sly glances throughout their first German lesson that term. She had been burning up all holiday with a mix of curiosity, envy and fury over the shocking possibility that Laura had actually been involved with their former German teacher. She had been even more irate at his sudden departure.

This term Teresa was determined to find out what had really been going on. She couldn't bear the thought that he had preferred Laura over her, as she had had a huge crush on him herself. But she had to know.

So she decided to call Laura's bluff.

"We all know why Mr Rydell left," she muttered to her when Frau Beinhof's back was turned.

"Do we?" Charlotte answered for Laura. She was always on high alert around their enemy, her ears missed nothing.

Frau Beinhof asked them to be silent so Teresa was forced to bite her tongue. She pinched her thin lips together, annoyed, and tossed her head to avoid looking at Charlotte. But she accosted them again right after class.

"I know what was going on between them. It was so obvious."

"As I think I said to you last term, why don't you take your concerns to Mrs Grayson? Whether she'll care about your unfounded allegations about a member of staff who doesn't even work here any more, well, all I can say is good luck to you. Come on Laura."

The three of them hurried away to the next class. Unfortunately Teresa would be in it as well, but there wasn't a lot they could do about that.

* * *

Lunch was an opportunity for some proper analysis of the morning and the term ahead. The four of them managed to sit at the far end of the table from the supervising teacher so they didn't have to mind their manners and make polite conversation, and could instead gossip undisturbed.

"So how was Geography?" Charlotte asked Susie as they picked the more edible lumps out of some sort of brown stew. It was served with beans that had once been green but were now soft and greyish, and boiled potatoes.

"It's going to be a breeze. After all that extra work I did last term, now someone is finally marking my work fairly I'm going to walk it," Susie said.

"That's not what I meant. I meant what's our new orienteering nemesis like?"

"He's alright. Not my type of course, if you mean in that regard, but he'll do for a Geography teacher." Susie liked her men a little more complicated and worldly. "He already has plenty of admirers as you can imagine, so he won't be short of volunteers to clean his blackboard. He's a bit wholesome for me so nothing for Darius to worry about there."

Margery was taken aback by Susie's blithe confidence that she could have attracted the new Geography teacher had she wanted to. She was still troubled about Laura and Mr Rydell, with her own father being a languages teacher it felt all the more wrong to her. "So you're still seeing Darius?" she asked, tucking into her stew.

"More or less."

Darius Iles was a prefect at St Duncan's, the brother-school to Francis Hall. Susie had started dating him after they met on a school trip to a local museum, with Charlotte ending up dating his friend Julian, the rugby captain of St Duncan's. School didn't really allow a lot of time for relationships. You could write letters and hope to meet if there was a shared school activity, but such events were rare.

This supposedly kept relationships on a more innocent, pen-pal level. In reality it meant that couples were so desperate to get some time together that they often leapfrogged several stages of dating as soon as they managed to be alone. You didn't waste time playing chess or enjoying casual conversation if you only had ten minutes behind the sports pavilion to further your acquaintance. Teachers rarely seemed to realise this though.

"I wonder if Mr Peters will be after you again this term," Charlotte said to Susie.

"If he's given up, it will be a relief, and if he hasn't, I'll just have to find some way to make it amusing," Susie said. She was already making plans for the term ahead. It was going to be a challenge topping last term's antics but she didn't doubt that she would manage it somehow.

At that moment they were interrupted by Teresa Hubert and her henchwomen who unfortunately took the next seats along. Teresa was also seething from her failure to get Susie into trouble last term.

Never one to miss an opportunity to dig, she got stuck in.

"Nice holiday then? I heard you all went gallivanting around Italy."

"It was quite lovely, thank you." The sweetness in Susie's tone masked deadly poison. Teresa was either too stupid to notice or too bold to care.

"You must be sad about losing your German teacher, Laura," Teresa said. She was still hoping to get some kind of reaction out of Laura but Charlotte answered for her.

"I don't know about you, Teresa, but we're finding Frau Beinhof an excellent replacement."

"No teacher can quite fully substitute in every area, can they?" Once again Teresa was directing her remark to Laura.

Laura did not rise to the bait. "I think it's an extra advantage, if anything, having a native speaker," she said.

"Better for oral, you mean?" One of Teresa's henchwomen sniggered at the joke.

"I'm sure you'd know best about that," Susie told her, "with all the crap that comes out of your mouth." She pointedly shifted so her shoulder was turned away from Teresa and started talking in Italian to the other three. None of them could really understand what she was saying, but Teresa didn't realise this. Laura managed to make a couple of Italian responses and Charlotte pitched in with what was essentially half Latin, half gibberish, but it was enough to confuse and annoy Teresa.

Later they were bent double with laughter recalling Teresa's furious face as they left the dining hall.

"We'll have to do that again, it was priceless," Charlotte said.

"If we all actually learned Italian it would make more sense," Margery pointed out.

Susie thought for a moment. "You're right, it would be incredibly useful to be able to talk privately in front of people. I would teach you, but there's far too much to do this term already. We'll just have to fake it when Teresa is around. It's just as much fun, and she'll never know."

* * *

They were all relieved when the first day was over and they were finally back in the privacy of the dorm, just the four of them. With the thick curtains drawn and the radiator cranked up to the highest setting it was also a lot more comfortable.

The start of term was always overwhelming: teachers loaded everyone up with homework and textbooks and it seemed like they would never scale the mountainous syllabus before the term ended.

"No school social events this term, no birthdays among any of us, nothing else remotely entertaining happening, it's going to be a hard task to squeeze some fun out of the next couple of months," Susie said. She was sitting cross-legged on her bed having already sorted out all her things.

Margery, who was re-folding some clothes that had got crumpled in her trunk, couldn't see why it mattered. "Can't we just focus on our studies? There's so much to get through as it is."

"Schoolwork alone is not enough," Susie told her. "We need more to stimulate our minds. If the world suddenly ends, I don't want to have spent my last month doing maths homework."

"If the world did end tomorrow, who would you want to be with?" Charlotte asked.

Susie tipped her head to one side. "Much as I adore all of you, it would have to be my parents. Preferably all of us together in Italy with my cousins. But then I'd feel bad about my English relatives, I suppose. It's hard having such a widespread family."

"I suppose I'd want to be with my family, all things considered," Charlotte said. "What about you, Margery?"

"My dad of course."

Laura wished Charlotte had never asked the question because she was genuinely torn. Loyalty made her feel that she should pick her family. But not to spend the last day on earth with Mr Rydell was an unbearable prospect.

She thought of all her family's faces. Imagined the hurt on them if she chose to spend Doomsday with someone else, someone they had never even met. But saying goodbye to him forever, even a day before it was necessary: she just couldn't do it.

"I'd have to get them all together. So we'd spend the last day of existence having a huge and awful row, I expect." The last day of her life would end up being the worst day of her life. You just couldn't win.

8. Orienteering

Their first orienteering expedition was an unmitigated disaster. It didn't help that in typical regimental fashion, and to avoid disputes, the school had determined that each group leader would be determined alphabetically. This put Charlotte in charge of their group of four, being surnamed Bevan, and poor Charlotte was about as competent at map-reading as she was at Swahili.

There hadn't been any hockey matches that first weekend which had been a relief. It also turned out that they wouldn't have to go orienteering every week, though Mr Hollier had announced his intentions to start a club for those who were extra keen. None of them planned to sign up.

Charlotte tried to delegate her map-reading responsibilities, but additional opinions only seemed to confuse things further. "Too many cooks," Susie remarked as they took a wrong turn yet again after arguing about which way to go.

They were supposed to be tracking down numbered markers in some remote area of woodland and wilderness. When you reached a marker, there was a hole-punch device attached. Each one made a different impression in a card you had to complete, so you couldn't fake finding the others by making pin-pricks. This had been clearly explained to them to dispel any ideas of cheating.

Instead of finding markers they were endlessly wandering around ferny, marshy, boggy areas trying to figure out which streams matched those on their Ordnance Survey map, and whether the compass was supposed to point south east to a pine wood or or north east to what might be deserted farm buildings.

It was hopeless. They were cold, lost and fed up and hadn't seen any other groups for hours. Damp undergrowth and stick mud had also leached the wet through their trainers.

"We must have made just one wrong turn somewhere," Margery said, trying to get things back on track. But her own cartography skills were even more pathetic than Charlotte's. Susie simply didn't care or not whether they found the markers, and Laura was a bit lost in one of her dream worlds. She had paid least attention to the map, assuming she wouldn't do any better than the others.

"I'll tell you what we'll do," Susie said, finally having had enough of rocks and trees. "We'll keep walking in a single direction until we find a road. We will eventually come to a road or the ends of the earth, and either would be better than this."

So they did so. It didn't take long to find a road, a typical country lane with high hedges and fields either side. It was an enormous relief just to be walking on dry tarmac again.

They could go east or west, and Susie flipped a coin for this. With her typical luck, after about ten minutes of walking they saw houses that turned out to be the start of a small village.

"We should phone for help," Margery said.

"Let's go for a drink first. We can at least warm up," Susie said. She had no intention of going straight back, not when there was a country pub just across the road. Besides which they weren't expected back at the coach for more than an hour. It would be a miracle if all the other groups made it back by then anyway.

Inside the pub it was lovely and warm with big wooden beams, open fireplaces and the usual cosy nooks. "If anyone asks, we're students from the local agricultural college," Susie instructed them before going in, "out doing land surveying, or counting sheep or something."

From the moment she turned on her charm with the barman, who probably was a student himself at the local college, there was no need for excuses or fake IDs. He was only too happy to serve their order - Margery stuck to lemonade - and the four girls tucked themselves around a table next to a log fire.

They were all relieved to be out of the cold, even Margery though she remained nervous and said that they should try to contact the school as soon as possible.

"Relax. They're not expecting us for hours, anyway."

They enjoyed a pleasant half hour or so seated around the table. They shared a couple of bags of crisps and had just been reminiscing about Italy and plotting other diversions for the term when Charlotte grabbed Laura and swore. "It's Mr Hollier."

The Geography teacher had entered the pub and seen them immediately. There was nothing they could do so Susie brazened it out.

"Hello Sir. We got horribly lost so we were just staving off hypothermia with a sit by the fire and a drink of lemonade."

"Lemonade?" He clearly didn't believe her.

"Yes, see." Susie pushed Margery's glass towards him.

"I suppose I had better check this." He sipped it, and passed it back, reassured. He didn't seem too angry which was a relief. Laura silently thanked Margery for choosing a soft drink, they all owed her one. As well as Susie's quick wits, though it was Susie who had got them into this predicament in the first place.

"So you're all enjoying your first orienteering expedition?" he asked them. Laura could see in his eyes that he knew the answer to this. He was smarter than they would have liked.

"Oh very greatly, thank you," Charlotte said.

"Glad to hear it. So I'll see your names all signed up for the Orienteering Club, then? I'm sure we won't need to worry the Head about your getting lost today, if you're all putting in some extra practice to make sure it doesn't happen again."

Blackmail. He had them over a barrel and he knew it. He was grinning at their poorly concealed dismay. Charlotte was in particular turmoil because of her hockey commitments. "And now I had better join you while you finish your drinks."

Laura thought he intended them to drink up immediately but instead he ordered a pint of his own at the bar and sat down with them. They were all sitting around a curved bench that went along the sides and back of the table. Mr Hollier took a chair. It felt as though he had taken the head of the table.

"So I don't know all your names yet. Except yours," he said, indicating Susie, "as you're in my Geography class. The rest of you do German?"

They gave him their names. He had already heard of Charlotte. "You're the one that plays hockey, right? In which case I'll let you off from joining Orienteering Club this time."

"I didn't realise joining the club was supposed to be a punishment," Susie said. "Is that why you're having to take conscripts?"

"I don't think you'll find it punishing when you get the hang of it," he told her.

"Like so many things in life." Susie was trying to get a rise out of him.

"What other things have you found less punishing after practice?" he asked her.

"The same ones as you, I expect." She looked at him very pointedly.

Laura blushed in embarrassment, unable to believe Susie was pushing things this far. Yet Susie wasn't even flirting with him. It was purely a game of wits. Charlotte wasn't entirely following and it was going completely over Margery's head.

Mr Hollier realised the conversation was about to cross a line. He changed the subject abruptly, after catching Laura's eye and seeing both discomfiture and sympathy there. He didn't know yet that no one beat Susie, ever. Nothing got to her: she was simply too quick, and she didn't care enough about anything.

They talked of other things for another half hour while they finished the drinks. Laura sensed that even Mr Hollier was reluctant to leave the fireside for the cold, damp outdoors. "I'll accompany you to the next marker and then point you in the direction of the next, so you can try and catch up. How many have you got so far?"

The answer was a single figure: one sole marker. He looked surprised but laughed. "Okay, I'll just take you to the nearest one and you can do your best. I'll expect to see a improvement in coming weeks. It's really not that hard once you get your head around the map symbols and get used to estimating distance and time."

Considering their progress so far Laura highly doubted this. She wondered if she could find some way to get out of it like Charlotte had done. Maybe if they did so badly at the first club meeting that they held everyone else up Mr Hollier would relent. Spending every Saturday out in the miserable winter weather was an appalling prospect.

* * *

"It might not be so bad," Charlotte said later. "He was pretty cool about us being in that pub. And I'm sure he guessed Margery was the only one drinking lemonade. Maybe he'll let you get up to some fun."

"I doubt it. And it's all very well for you to say so, you're not the one who'll be dumped in the woods in the pouring rain with only a compass," Laura said.

Susie, as ever, was irrepressible. "We'll just have to make our own fun. Besides, I had detention every single Saturday last term anyway so it's not much change for me."

For Laura it meant the loss of precious reading time, but lately she had found it hard to concentrate. She kept drifting into thoughts of Mr Rydell every time she tried to lose herself in a novel.

Margery was the most upset. "I desperately needed that time to study. I'm going to see if Gi-Gi can sort it out."

Laura privately rated Margery's chances with their housemistress as very low. In her experience teachers were endlessly keen for them to be pushed into as many outdoor activities as possible. "Fresh air" was a constant refrain.

"Don't worry Margie, we'll fix it somehow," Susie told her. She had a malevolent gleam in her eye.

Laura suspected she planned to try and torment Mr Hollier until he kicked them all out in desperation. Even if she failed in this - and Laura thought she probably would, as the new Geography teacher had more mettle than first realised - Susie would wrest some victory from it. She always won. At the very least it would be diverting to see what she got up to this time.

* * *

Later that week Susie got a letter from Italy in a scrawled envelope. She frowned, then laughed. "This is for you!"

She handed another envelope to Laura. "It's from Mr Rydell. He sent it via Ferdinando. You should have got it days ago but my cousin is so disorganised he only just posted it."

Laura opened it. It was brief, dated the day of their departure in Italy and on notepaper from the hotel they had stayed at.

My darling,

It seemed safer to send you a letter this way.

The past week has been incredible. It's only two hours since you left but looking at the empty bed I'm already regretting letting you go. If I was only marginally more selfish I would have made you stay with me, and to hell with everything.

Pflanze auf meine Lenden
Deiner Liebesküsse Raserei

There is much more I'd like to write but my flight leaves soon and I have to give this to Susie's cousin. Let's hope he remembers to post it, and quickly.

I love you beyond words.

PS Don't let the new German teacher translate the above.

It was the first letter he had ever written her, except for a note he had once slipped inside her exercise book. Laura was going to need a dictionary but the image of the bed and the remembrance of their time there made her blush.

"No need to ask what he wrote to you," Susie said. "It's written all over your face."

Laura smiled. The day was less bleak now. Even the cold and the encroaching dark of evening seemed brighter and warmer. She wondered how she could reply to him. She had an address for him but she couldn't risk someone seeing his name on the envelope in the school post. If she put a fake name would the post office still deliver it?

9. Phone call

The cold seemed to creep around them that term, hand in hand with the darkness. Even though it was several weeks past the winter solstice and the days were slowly getting longer, there never seemed to be enough light.

Even Charlotte complained of the freezing, dark mornings when she rose before dawn to go running. There seemed to be so many demands and activities that term that the only spare time she could be certain of was in the early morning. This training wasn't required but she felt it gave her an edge. She was the youngest player on the hockey team and she sometimes felt the lack of the two extra years of playing that older girls had.

Occasionally a teammate would come running with her but usually Charlotte exercised alone. It meant creeping out of the dorm down the draughty stairs of Michaelmas Hall - the central heating was switched on around the same time, but didn't yet take effect - and going outside into the freezing night air. Sometimes it was so cold it made her gasp. But she felt at one with the world, it was her own time and space.

"I can't believe Charlotte drags herself out of bed so early on mornings like these," Laura said as she came back from the bathroom, already shivering. She could have stayed in the hot shower all day. It was practically the only time she felt properly warm.

"I heard Grace Grant say they were going to increase the heating," Margery told her. "Apparently they didn't expect temperatures to be this low."

"It's definitely colder than last year."

Laura longed for spring. For green shoots, daffodils, that sweet sharp strain of perfume that all spring flowers seemed to share regardless of their variety.

* * *

Laura managed to make an undisturbed phone call to Mr Rydell that night. He wanted to be able to call her but there was a danger that someone receiving the call might recognise his voice. The payphone was on the way to Grace Grant's office so she was often the one to answer it if no girls were around.

Even if he had disguised his voice, with Miss Grant already having guessed the situation, it would look obvious if an odd-sounding "cousin" suddenly rang for Laura. So it fell to her to call him. He was travelling a lot at the moment with his new job and while he tried to give her contact numbers and dates when he wrote, it was hard.

So managing to get through finally, and hear his voice, was rare and wonderful.

"How have you been?"

"Freezing cold. Missing you."

"I know exactly how I would warm you up," he told her and proceeded to give her details. Laura stood there, melting with desire at the things he was telling her, trying to keep her face straight and desperately hoping no one would come past.

He hadn't spoken to her like this before. It shocked her but she loved it. He was telling her what he would do with his hands, what he would make her do with her body, how she would feel. He knew that she couldn't reciprocate as she didn't enjoy the same privacy at the end of the line as he did, and knowing this turned them both on.

He knew she was struggling to keep her control as he drove her wild with just his voice and the things he said.

"I want you so badly," she managed to whisper when she was sure there was no one around. How was she going to wait until half term for him?

He was so commanding and yet so concerned with her own feelings. And he knew her so well, or seemed to. Yet she often felt that she still didn't know a lot about him. That he had this past, all these years that made him who he was, that she couldn't ever equal.

They couldn't speak for too long. She had reversed the charges but there would be other girls queuing up to use the phone.

"I would put this in a letter to you," he said, "except your housemistress might get hold of it if I send it directly. Does she read German?"

"I don't think so, but nor do I when it comes to the kinds of things you're saying." She sensed his amusement on the other end.

"I might try it some time," he said.

"Don't." If a letter got intercepted and taken to Frau Beinhof for translation the results would be beyond mortifying. Besides which Grace Grant would instantly know who was writing to Laura anyway if she started getting letters in German. Letters were supposed to be private but once in a while there were checks. It had been risky enough for him to send that first letter via Ferdinando.

"What would you like to do at half term? I'm getting time off so we can go somewhere if you'd like."

What Laura wanted was simply to be with him somewhere warm, just him alone, uninterrupted.

"That shouldn't be a problem," he said. "What's the issue with being warm, is it very cold there?"

"They've switched off the heating or something, we're all dying of cold." The backs of her hands had become chapped and she was constantly rubbing lip balm into them to soothe her skin.

"If you're wearing the same underwear you wore in Italy I'm not surprised."

The exquisite lingerie that Susie had given her as a present had ended up as something of a problem for Laura. She couldn't leave it at home because if her mother had found it she would have freaked out. She couldn't wear it at school or hide it among her school clothes as Matron would have had a heart attack. She was too embarrassed to give it to Mr Rydell for safe keeping.

In the end she had asked Susie for advice. In typical fashion Susie had laughed and revealed a hidden area in the base of her trunk. "We'll put it here." The space had been designed for smuggling cigarettes and other substances by its previous owner, one of her cousins. Her parents had expected her to have a new school trunk but Susie had claimed her cousin's one was "lucky". She had used some glue to stick the lining of the trunk back down so there was no way that Matron, even if the she had the time or the inclination to pry, would find it.

Laura hadn't told Mr Rydell any of this. It seemed too silly, to be stressed about hiding a bra.

"How's my replacement?" he asked her. "Is he managing to inspire the same passion for German?"

Mr Rydell's heartthrob status had encouraged an unprecedented amount of eagerness to study German among the girls of Francis Hall during the previous term.

Laura could hear an edge in his voice, which along with the assumption of "he" revealed more than he probably intended.

"Not quite the same level, but it's still good. And it's a she, some old friend of Mrs Grayson."

She could tell he was relieved though he didn't admit it. She decided it would be wisest not to tell him about Mrs Ayers' replacement. Mr Hollier had already been established as the new pin-up of the school, though admittedly in a milder way than Mr Rydell had been. There was already considerably more enthusiasm for Geography than there had been under Mrs Ayers' reign of terror.

He probably wouldn't find it amusing to hear about them drinking in a pub with the new Geography teacher. Even though Mr Rydell was the one with the whole world at his access and Laura was effectively locked up at an all girls' boarding school, he was always strangely possessive about her. Which she loved. It made her feel safe, that she was still his.

He had nothing to worry about on her side. No one existed in the world except him, not like that.

* * *

Teresa Hubert, everyone's nemesis, was still seething with rage over her lack of victories the previous term. She had failed to win Margery's loyalty despite doing favours for her. She had been thwarted in her plans to sneak to Miss Grant, when she was sure she had seen Susie making a clandestine visit to Mr Rydell.

The final insult had been discovering on the very last day of term that Laura had enjoyed a much closer level of friendship with the German teacher than she herself had managed. Like many other girls at Francis Hall, Teresa had been struck by the devastatingly handsome teacher and had serious hopes of one day winning him.

She had fantasised about him confessing his hidden love to her on her final day of school, once it was safe for their love to be open, and walking off into the sunset with him.

Instead she had been forced to confront the fact that others enjoyed far warmer relationships with him than she did. It rankled. She still wasn't convinced, or couldn't bear to admit, that Laura and Mr Rydell had gone beyond "discussing Goethe" but he'd certainly never offered extra poetry lessons to Teresa.

So she was on their case this term. The gruesome foursome, as she thought of them. Every phone call Laura got, or any letters that arrived for any of them, Teresa had got her beady eye on.

"Spying again?" Susie said, catching Teresa peering over at a letter she was carrying.

"Hardly. As if I'd be interested in anything that you do."

Teresa was also kicking herself for having chosen German when the Geography students were now the ones with the handsome new teacher.

Which meant that odious Susie Clarke got to sit in his classes and be all over him for orienteering. Teresa was in the Lower School hockey team so she played matches most Saturdays. She would have been thrilled with this except it now reduced her chances to do orienteering and try and ingratiate herself with Mr Hollier.

Teresa boiled with resentment. She was certain they laughed at her behind her back. Somehow, she would get even with them.

10. Navigating

Of all the terms to have ended up forced into an outdoor activity it would have to be this one. Mr Poynter's bookbinding club would have been preferable: at least you got to sit in the library which was kept reasonably warm. After all the books would be ruined if they got damp, pupils, however, were considered significantly more robust.

"You can warm up afterwards with a hot bath," Matron had told one girl making exaggerated complaints of frostbite.

The school heating really seemed to have been turned down a notch that term. There were endless grumbles about it. Laura actually found herself sending home for thermal vests, usually unheard of as they were considered frumpy garments that only people's grandmothers wore.

"Maybe Francis Hall is going bankrupt," Charlotte said. "Or maybe Mrs Grayson is hoarding the coal money for ill gotten gains."

Either way it made being in the woods marginally more bearable. In the second half of term they had to go on an actual camping expedition as part of the Duke of Edinburgh award and sleep out overnight in tents. Everyone was dreading it.

"Cornwall in summer would be great," Laura said. "But not the moors in winter."

With Charlotte playing hockey the leadership duties for the Orienteering Club foursome fell on Laura as her surname preceded Susie's and Margery's. Due to her absence they had needed a fourth and managed to a recruit a short, quiet girl called Mary Rudge.

Wearing jeans and their warmest clothes - fortunately they weren't required to wear school uniform, as sports kit was sent to the laundry on Saturdays for those who weren't playing matches - they shuffled onto the school coach.

"It's like we're being herded to the gulags," Susie said. "Driven into the middle of nowhere and dumped."

Mr Hollier overheard, as she had intended him to.

"There's considerably less barbed wire. And fewer armed guards," he told her.

"There was plenty of barbed wire last time. I snagged my jumper on it," another girl complained.

He drew out an ordnance survey map. "See that symbol there? It's a stile. Try finding one next time."

They weren't the only ones that had been coerced into this. Mr Hollier had used orienteering as an alternative to detention for several girls in his Geography classes.

"At least press gangs got the King's Shilling," Susie had commented.

Mr Hollier looked at her, reached into his pocket and drew out a coin. He offered it to Susie who did not take it. "You see? I refuse to take it. Now I should be absolved," she told him.

Laura was starting to feel slightly sorry for Mr Hollier. While he seemed to be shrugging it off it couldn't have been much fun for him that everyone was so reluctant and complaining about something he clearly enjoyed.

They reached the drop off point which was by a farm gate. Hearts sank with feet into the mud as they got out and formed into their groups.

Laura could have been curled up in the Common Room at Michaelmas House, reading a book right now. With a hot mug of tea and biscuits if any could be pinched from somewhere. Out of the damp air and the biting wind. Anywhere but here.

Maps, compasses and punch cards were handed out and Laura took charge of the ones for her group. Mary Rudge, amazingly, had actually signed up for this voluntarily. She came from a farming family and liked the outdoors even though she was hopeless at sports.

"I know I'm supposed to be leader," Laura told the others, "but I honestly have no clue what I'm doing. If any of you want to give this a go, be my guest."

No one did. "It was like Greek to me last time," Susie said. Margery had fared no better and Mary was too timid to put herself forward. So it fell on Laura to try and get them on the right route.

She unfolded the map and refolded it so she could see the current section they were on. "This is the starting point." That was helpfully marked on the map for them. "Now we have to head sort of north west, I think, to the first marker. Which is towards that hill." She rotated the map around to check.

Once she actually gave it her attention, Laura was surprised to find that map-reading was both easy and enjoyable. It seemed to fit together in her head somehow, she could look at the landscape and then see it on the map. She quickly got a sense of judging distance: of how long walking across a particular kind of terrain would look on the map.

It would have been easier if the day wasn't overcast as the sun would have given them a better sense of east and west. But even without shadows to help them, it wasn't as bad as she had feared.

If the others had all been as fit as Charlotte they might have made lightning fast progress. But even last term's cross country training had had its limits, and they trekked between the checkpoints instead of running. With Laura's navigation it was still enough for them to come in first, comfortably ahead of the next team.

Mr Hollier was surprised and impressed. He scrutinised their card in case there had been shenanigans with fake hole punching, but everything was in order.

"I just got the hang of it or something," Laura said.

"You certainly did." They all won Mars Bars as the prize for coming in first, and chatted to him while they waited for all the rest of the teams to arrive. They learned that Francis Hall was only his second job after teacher training college and Laura calculated that he must be about twenty-five.

Susie still tried to rile him but was better behaved than last time. Partly because she genuinely liked him - though anyone would have seemed delightful in contrast to Mrs Ayers - and partly because she had realised he had more intellectual substance than she had initially assumed.

Even if he lacked the languid cynicism of Darius and the kinds of guys Susie usually liked, or the dark sardonic humour of Mr Rydell, he was no walkover. Unlike so many of the other girls Susie didn't have any romantic regard for him, he was too outdoors and uncomplicated for that, but she liked him nonetheless.

The main reason, though, that Susie was behaving better was because she already had some other plans for the exeat weekend that were occupying the more calculating part of her mind. She hadn't discussed these plans with Charlotte and Laura yet - she didn't even consider telling Margery as she knew any attempts to get her along would be futile - but she was fairly decided about what she wanted to do. And it would be more fun, and possibly easier, to have both Charlotte and Laura along.

"Perhaps in future weeks we should wait somewhere inside, in the warm," Susie suggested. "Like last time. It might be a nice incentive for people to hurry up and finish."

"By all means," Mr Hollier said, surprising her. "If you can find a café rather than a licensed premises."

Susie's face, which had momentarily shown surprise and hope, fell. Laura knew this was an act. Susie couldn't care less what he did or did not allow.

But she played along. "I don't think crisps and lemonade in a nice country pub would be problematic, do you, Sir?"

"I'm happy to put the suggestion to Mrs Grayson."

Susie, still acting, scowled. "We don't need to bother her. I'm sure she'll be happy enough that we're all out getting some fresh air."

"Then she'll be even more delighted if you remain outside to get the maximum fresh air." Mr Hollier wasn't going to give an inch. They had no chance of persuading him to greenlight them spending Saturday afternoons in a pub.

* * *

"No way!" Charlotte said when Susie finally revealed her plans for exeat weekend.

Susie wanted to go clubbing in London, to one of the top nightclubs, and party until dawn. "The beauty is that we don't even have to worry about where we stay. We'll be up all night."

The logistics of getting away weren't so much of a problem. They could tell their parents they were staying over at one another's houses. Laura rarely went home for exeats anyway as Cornwall was too far to travel to for a single night.

"Wouldn't we need ID to get in?" Laura asked.

"Maybe, maybe not. We'll get in somewhere. If we look the part they'll let us straight in, no questions."

Susie didn't tell them what she knew from her limited experience of clubbing in London with her cousins: that being under the required entry age would be an advantage, being girls. All the famous "wild child" starlets on the London scene that dated pop stars were in their teens. They were constantly in the tabloids, partying, dancing on tables. One girl had even eloped to Las Vegas with a rockstar at the age of fifteen.

So Susie wasn't concerned about that. She just had to figure out a few things such as changing their clothes, but that was all easy to arrange. Fortunately they had the frocks from Italy which would be ideal for nightclubs: this had been at the back of Susie's mind when she helped choose them.

She owned a little designer number herself stashed in her trunk which Matron had noticed and pursed her lips at, but there wasn't a lot she could do. Unless Susie tried to wear it to Sunday chapel it wasn't breaking the rules to simply have such a garment with her. Matron might complain to Grace Grant but the housemistress had already witnessed Susie's exotic wardrobe at the school dance last year, so she wouldn't be shocked.

It wasn't like Laura's Italian lingerie which might have got mentioned to her parents. Underwear like that was a world away from a minidress. Susie grinned just thinking about it all.

They could probably do with heels, she thought, as the extra height might help them past the doormen, but they could have a fun afternoon shopping for those.

Mentally she rubbed her hands together. It was all decided. This would be so much more exciting than her illicit midnight party the term before, and much safer. They would be on leave from school and far away from school grounds.

The thought of bumping into a member of staff in Tramps or Annabel's was happily absurd. Susie indulged a little fantasy of encountering Mrs Grayson on the dancefloor and the others had to ask her why she was smiling.

11. The snow

As soon as the cold eased a fraction it snowed. Thick and soft, it covered the playing fields and the school roof and the black boughs of trees. It awoke a new spirit in everyone: it was like a return to childhood. There were snowball fights and ice slides and just as quickly notices in assembly about penalties for the same.

"They never want us to have any fun," Charlotte said.

"You'd regret it if you slipped and cracked an ankle," Margery told her. "You'd be off hockey for the rest of the year."

Uniform rules were partially relaxed when it came to winter clothing. The school shop had sold out of regulation maroon hats, gloves and scarves so non uniform ones were allowed. The different colours clashed horribly with the school maroon but they lifted people's spirits.

Hot cocoa, or something approximating it, was also doled out at break time. It was so watered down that it served better as a handwarmer than a drink but it was better than nothing.

"It tastes of burnt," Laura said and the phrase caught on. "A cup of burnt" became its new description.

They were fed up with the staff making cheery comments as they passed them in the courtyard. Pupils were still herded out as often as possible for their dose of fresh air, whereas there were suspicions of more than adequate heating in the staff room.

"A roaring log fire," Susie said. "They sit around it roasting chestnuts. I'm sure I could smell mulled wine when Mr Poynter was breathing over my shoulder in History."

"We'd see the smoke from the chimney if they had a log fire. I've seen the inside of the staff room before, they just have a little gas heater like the ones everywhere," Charlotte told her.

"Cranked up to the highest heat, I expect, unlike the ones everywhere else."

Games were cancelled at the height of the snow though orienteering was kept up. Somehow Mr Hollier had ended up called Tom outside school, even to his face. Laura wasn't sure how it had started. It eventually spilled over behind his back in school as well. People referred to him as "Tom" but as "Mr Hollier" in class.

It wasn't without precedent: they had always referred to their housemistress as Grace Grant. It said something about the accessibility of certain teachers, Laura thought. Whereas no one would even think of Mrs Grayson as "Eleanor".

Tom Hollier, for his part, didn't seem to care. So long as the proper formalities were observed in school he was happy to relax them for orienteering club. The girls called him a mix of Tom and Sir, which should have been incongruous but just seemed to fit.

Only Margery, who was a stickler for tradition, avoided calling him by his first name. "Why do you keep tormenting Mr Hollier?" she asked Susie. "Or trying to torment him, since I don't think it's working."

"Tom can take it. I only do it because he pushes back," Susie told her.

"He might get the wrong impression. Some of the things you say are really suggestive," Margery said.

Susie laughed. "Trust me, if I had any genuine designs on him he wouldn't know what had hit him. I wouldn't be joking around with him in an obvious way if I had those kind of plans."

"He might not know that though." Margery was worried about it, particularly after what had happened between Laura and Mr Rydell the previous term. Susie constantly had sparring matches with Mr Hollier and they seemed to be getting more and more outrageous. She shuddered to think what Susie got up to in his Geography classes.

"I think Tom's pretty astute," Susie said, to reassure her. "Besides if I felt any vibe like that from him, I'd stop immediately. One Mr Peters is quite enough to cope with."

Mr Peters, the Head of English, whose amorous advances to Susie had become an increasing bore the previous term, was fortunately less of a problem this term. His close shave in the ghastly encounter with Mrs Ayers - when he'd expected to seduce Susie with champagne and erotic poetry, but had instead ended up half naked and harangued by the deranged former Geography teacher - had severely shaken his spirit. He was still reeling when the new term came around.

His vanity was such that it didn't for a moment cross his mind that his "beloved Susanna" had orchestrated the mishap. But he'd lost his nerve for now, and he consoled himself by thinking that Susie was probably too young and shy for the kind of affaire he had in mind, and it would be better to focus his attentions elsewhere.

Mr Peters still mooned after her in class and ensured that she read the part of any Shakespearean character with saucy lines to say. But he hadn't pressed his offers of private coaching any further, nor sought her out around the school grounds after class.

Susie, for her part, was relieved. She was used to male attention, desirable or otherwise, it didn't scare or intimidate her. But Mr Peters had become a creepy bore. A useful creepy bore, of course, who had played right into her hands in the final destruction of Mrs Ayers last term.

She now had mixed feelings about the destruction of Mrs Ayers. Not in terms of any sympathy for Mrs Ayers or any sense of guilt in accelerating her towards a nervous breakdown, but because the Geography teacher's absence left her without a campaign. She didn't need an enemy, per se, but she enjoyed the machinations of battle. It was partly why she tried to rile Tom Hollier but that was more of a joke. It was too overt and too well received to give Susie any real satisfaction.

"I find myself missing the Axe at times," she said, using Mrs Ayers' nickname. "Geography classes just aren't the same when I come top every week and actually get nice comments on my homework."

"It's your fault she left. You drove her to it," Charlotte said. They were sitting in the courtyard, shivering over their steaming cups of burnt watery cocoa.

"I was the lightest straw, the merest final wisp that broke that camel," Susie told her. "And let's face it, I did her a favour. She

73

needed a break. She'll doubtless come back next year as sweet as pie, begging me to do A-level Geography."

Even Margery doubted this. The Geography teacher's absence made little difference to her, though, as she had swapped Geography for German.

"It will be a popular A-level next year if Tom stays around," Charlotte said.

Grace Grant passed them in the courtyard and nodded as she went past. She liked the four of them very much but they also troubled her. In particular she still wasn't quite sure what she felt about Susie Clarke.

She had expected the half-Italian girl to be a troublemaker when she arrived last term. Already effectively expelled from several schools, she anticipated a defiant girl, someone curt with staff, badly behaved and resistant to punishment.

Instead Susie had turned out to be a very bright, very charming girl who ostensibly played carefully by the rules. Grace Grant was not so naive as to think that Susie didn't raise various kinds of hell when teachers' backs were turned.

But the episode between the schoolgirl and Mrs Ayers had been both unexpected and disconcerting. Susie had held the upper hand all the way despite observing every rule and penalty meted out by her teacher.

She was such a likeable girl. Generous, loyal to her friends. Grace Grant had kept a close eye on Susie's three dorm mates but failed to see any detrimental effects from Susie's companionship. On the contrary, since Susie's arrival Charlotte Bevan had started excelling at hockey, Laura Cardew was suddenly writing English essays of a startling quality and maturity, and Margery had topped the language classes at the end of last term by a mile.

Of course these things couldn't be directly attributed to Susie, or indeed attributed to her at all. But they certainly disavowed any negative influence that Grace Grant might have feared.

The housemistress still had her eye on Laura. She remained concerned about the possible relationship that had developed between her and the German teacher, Mr Rydell. She had no proof but it had been written all over both their faces when she observed them at the poetry recital last year. She had also had a talk with

Laura about it, and was fairly certain that Laura had understood what she was trying to say.

She wondered how the relationship had developed between them. Laura was not a sultry or flirtatious type of girl, not the kind to send love notes to a male teacher let alone fling herself at him. And Mr Rydell had seemed an intelligent and worldly young man, not a nascent Mr Peters. The German teacher had certainly dealt with the more obvious yearnings of other pupils with tact and humour.

So why had he crossed the line with Laura? And how far had it gone? Grace Grant hoped it had been nothing too involved, after all, he was nearly twice her age. He should have been aware of the impropriety and the risks involved.

Such a liaison could not end happily and she was relieved that he had left. Most probably on account of his inappropriate feelings, she thought. At least it showed the man had some sense and conscience. Less sense than Eleanor Grayson these days, in Grace Grant's view, continually employing such handsome young men to teach boy-starved boarding school girls. God only knew what Tom Hollier was having to put up with.

Grace Grant thought - hoped - that Mr Rydell's leaving meant any relationship which had developed between Laura and him was now over.

She also remembered Susie's odd behaviour regarding the former German teacher. The housemistress still wasn't sure what exactly lay behind Susie's absurd confession - that she had tried and failed to seduce Mr Rydell - but she suspected it was some kind of cover up for Laura. Susie was like that. It was as admirable a quality as it was frustrating at times, at least for a teacher trying to get at the truth.

Grace Grant remembered the girls' school stories she had read in her youth, when "honour" was paramount and "sneaking" was an evil worse than murder.

Odd how Susie Clarke, with her modern sophistication and precocious wiles, somehow fitted that template more than any of the rest of the girls.

PART II

Playing

Open the door of thy heart,
And open thy chamber door,
And my kisses shall teach thy lips
The love that shall fade no more

Bedouin Song, Bayard Taylor

12. First exeat

The first exeat finally arrived and with it Susie's plans for an illicit night of clubbing in London. They had invited Margery knowing that she would probably refuse, which she did, so it was just the three of them.

The dresses that Susie had given them were bundled up into their bags. "We'll have to sort out shoes and other stuff. Our coats are black, they'll be fine," Susie said.

Departing from school presented the only real challenge. Because they were supposed to be being picked up by someone's parents it was awkward just to walk out on foot. They were taking the train and the station was only a mile or so walk from the school, but none of the three of them were supposed to be heading that way.

Fortunately Susie, detail-oriented as always, had figured this one out. Little Mary Rudge, their orienteering teammate, was getting picked up by her older brother. "We'll have him drop us down at the station. That way if we make it on time, we'll catch the earlier train and leave even before those people who are walking to the station." Susie had obtained a rail timetable and worked it all out. She would never suffer her plans to fail on a minor detail.

Both Charlotte and Laura were excited about the scheme. It didn't feel nearly as dangerous as Susie's midnight feast last term as at least it was off school grounds. It probably still broke school rules but who would know? Actually having boys and booze at Francis Hall in the middle of the night was catastrophically risky by comparison.

This was a breeze. They were also buoyed up by their time in Calabria, where they had been nightclubbing for the first time and experienced the kind of male attention one could get.

Mary was only too happy to oblige. She was grateful to them for teaming up with her for orienteering as normally she was one of the girls who got picked last. She also hugely admired Susie and was happy to be able to be useful to her.

"We owe you one, Mary," Susie told her. She meant it. Susie never forgot her debts, it was something she had learnt from her Italian relatives. Her supposed Machiavellian streak. Everything was leverage and all debts must be paid.

Mary's brother had finished at St Duncan's a couple of years before and was now at university. Susie was at her most charming so by the end of the ride he felt like he had been graced with her presence, not done her a favour.

They rushed to buy their tickets and managed to get the early London train that they wanted. Sitting on it, Susie devised a game to get any last nerves or doubt out of their systems.

"You need to imagine the most appalling thing that could happen, and then it won't happen. I used to do this with monsters under my bed. If I could imagine them then they couldn't be real, because it would be too much of a coincidence," she said.

Charlotte chose bumping into Miss Partridge, their hockey coach, on the dance floor. "That would be it for me, I'd never get to play on the team again."

"I highly doubt that," Susie said. "She's not going to put out an inferior team just because she caught the star player misbehaving. You might have to buy her silence though."

"I'm hardly the star player. I only hang on to my place because no one else likes playing on the left wing," Charlotte told her.

Laura imagined something even worse. "You'll be dancing," she told Susie, "and just like that club in Reggio you'll feel some guy grinding behind you. But when you turn round it won't be some hot guy like your friend Gio. It will be Mr Peters."

"With his flies undone," said Charlotte, picking up the theme, "and all sweaty."

"Wearing a black satin shirt with his chest hair showing."

"With his crotch all bulging and breathing cigarette breath all over you."

"Enough!" Susie said. "I doubt he's got enough to bulge anyway. Here's mine: the headmistress, in a lycra boob tube. Dirty dancing... with your father."

This was addressed to Charlotte whose father was notoriously strict. "I almost wish that would happen," she said. "I could hold it over him and do what I wanted for the rest of eternity."

"Once you go to university it will be a lot easier," Laura said. "He'll be off your back. You'll be an independent adult. Even if he kicks you out of home in the holidays you can always come and stay with me."

The plan was to go to Oxford Street, where they would still have an hour or so before the shops closed. They could buy some shoes and other things and change. Susie said they could leave their bags at a hotel cloakroom. "You don't have to actually be staying there, some of them will just accept bags for a quid or so. Or you just give them a fake room number if they ask."

Then they would go out to eat and for a wander around the place, maybe to a bar. Then when it was late enough they would find their way to one of the major nightclubs and hopefully get past the bouncers.

Susie didn't appear to have a contingency plan for if they were turned away, other than trying other clubs. Actually if they got stuck she would just put them up at a hotel on the credit card her uncle had given her, but she didn't want them to consider this an option yet in case they lost their nerve for trying to get into somewhere else.

Ideally if she had had more time and ability to plan she would have contrived to get their names on a guest list somewhere. But that was hard enough to do without trying to coordinate it from Francis Hall. She was too out of the loop stuck away at school.

* * *

"These heels are way too high, I can barely walk," Charlotte said. "Plus it's not as though I need the height."

Susie had already made them change into their little black dresses so they could properly see what the shoes they were trying would look like.

"It's not about height, it's about dress code. I mean dressing like everyone else does, so you look the part. High heels will help make you look older."

Charlotte tried walking in her shoes once more, doing an exaggerated catwalk strut across the shop. She tripped and collapsed laughing against Laura after a few paces. She nearly knocked a woman over and had to apologise. The woman gave her a keen look but didn't say anything.

"We'll practise some more on the way to dinner," Susie said.

"A fine sight we'll look, tottering down the road like clowns on stilts."

Susie had bought a cheap pair of heels that looked precipitously high, but managed to walk in them as though she had been born in them. "It's very easy once you get the hang of it."

The three girls left the shop laden with shoeboxes, Laura and Charlotte relieved to be back in their school shoes for a moment, even if they looked absurdly frumpy paired with the designer frocks.

Outside someone tapped Charlotte on the arm. "Excuse me."

It was the woman she had collided with in the shoe shop. Charlotte braced herself for a dressing down.

Instead the woman handed her a business card. "Barbara Banks," she said. She was in her late forties or early fifties, she had a preserved, expensive look that reminded Laura of some of the rich women they had seen in Italy. Her coat looked designer and her hair was flawlessly cut and coloured. "If you're interested in trying modelling, give me a call. I have an appointment so I can't stop and chat now, but my assistant will arrange everything."

They were all taken aback. "It's probably dodgy," Charlotte said, not wanting to seem vain.

"Give me a look." Susie took the card and raised her eyebrows. "I don't think this is dodgy. It's one of the top agencies. She looked quite senior too."

"Will you call her?" Laura asked.

Charlotte had no idea what she would do. She was still in shock.

"It's because you're so tall," Susie said. "I don't mean you're not pretty as well, but in those heels you kind of look like a supermodel."

"All that running too," Laura said. "You've got so skinny."

"I'm actually heavier than I was six months ago."

"Yes, but it's muscle or whatever. You're really fit and tall, just like they are in magazines."

Charlotte looked downcast. "My father would never allow it. What with school and everything."

"He needn't know, at least at the start. Once you've signed a multimillion dollar deal to be the face of Chanel I'll bet he'll come around," Susie said.

They were all getting ahead of themselves and Charlotte knew it, but it was nice to fantasise.

It became a bit of a joke throughout the evening. "No pizza for you or you won't fit into the sample sizes in Milan," Susie said when their food arrived.

"I can't seriously ring her, can I? I'm at school and everything."

"You can't not ring her. Imagine getting handed an opportunity like that and never knowing what might have happened," Laura said.

"Besides she'll expect you to be at school. Many models start from fourteen or younger. You're practically geriatric," Susie told her.

"An old hag." Laura backed her up.

"A wizened old crone."

"Mrs Ayer's grandmother."

Charlotte stopped them. "Okay. I'll call. But I'll need some moral support."

Susie handed her an imaginary plate. "Have a platterful. And don't think I'm being unselfish, just think what kind of doors will open for all of us once you start hobnobbing with the rich and famous."

13. Clubbing

The excitement of the affair gave them all extra sparkle, and once they were dressed up and made up and could convincingly teeter at least ten paces in their heels, they easily got in to the first nightclub they tried.

Laura had no real idea what to expect. It seemed far bigger, more crowded and louder than the clubs in Reggio. She mentioned this to Susie.

"Well Reggio is hardly Rome, and it was low season," Susie told her.

They made their way to a bar which felt like clawing their way through a jungle of bodies. The noise level was immense, as well as the contrast with the brilliantly strobing lights on the dance floor and the shadowy black edges of the room.

They passed a roped off sign to a VIP area. "We'll be in there by the end of the night," Susie said.

There were just so many people. Laura knew London was huge, but it was hard to anticipate just how many cool, attractive, well dressed people there would be. There were also lots of other girls whom she suspected were younger than the entry age, as they were.

They let Susie order drinks as they were too overawed to know what to ask for. Susie handed them glasses. "It's some sort of cocktail. Don't worry about money as it's all going on my card." She knew the prices would likely shock them and she didn't want it to spoil the fun of the night.

It was so crowded it was impossible to find anywhere to put their drinks down so they held them. Laura watched the dance floor. At least people pretty much danced the same anywhere you went. She imagined gatecrashing a dance in Jane Austen's era and not having a clue what the moves were.

Laura wasn't exactly sure what Susie's intentions were when it came to getting approached at the club. If Susie and Charlotte hooked up with guys then she would be left a bit stranded. There was literally no one else in the world for her except Mr Rydell. She was still intoxicated by him in a way that Charlotte didn't seem to be with Julian, nor Susie with Darius. Though she hadn't actually observed Susie flirting particularly with anyone else, even in Italy.

"Let's dance," Charlotte said. She had to gesture because the music was so loud that conversation was impossible.

They navigated their way to the mass of moving bodies and dissolved themselves into the throng. Laura was more buzzed by adrenalin than from her drink, but either way it helped her lose herself. People swayed, twisted, gyrated. Underneath the beat drummed relentlessly. Sure enough there were guys that tried to dance against her but she managed to shake them off with a smile and turn away.

After a while the rhythm was hypnotising. The strobing lights, lasers, a smoke machine. That strange, burnt, dusty smell. It took ages to dissipate even after the smoke had cleared.

But she loved it. They all did. Something about the swirls of smoke turned it into a playground, for a moment everyone was simply having fun and not longer showing off, posing, trying to act alluring.

Laura wasn't eyeing up guys standing around but Susie and Charlotte were. Even though they had competition here - the place was packed with attractive girls - they still stood out. Charlotte was like a beacon with her height and her blonde hair. It was really her night, and Laura was glad for her.

She hoped the modelling might go somewhere, it would be so exciting for Charlotte and for the rest of them as her friends if anything actually happened.

They took a break. Before they could get more drinks, as they passed outside the VIP area, Susie nudged them. "Look!" Laura did so, and saw a man with streaked blond hair, surrounded by a large contingent of people, especially females. You could instantly tell he was the main person there, even though there were other men of similar age and style around him.

It took Laura a moment but she suddenly recognised him, as did Charlotte. It was the oddest feeling seeing someone just a few yards away whom you normally saw all over the covers of magazines.

"My god!" Charlotte was jabbing her in excitement. "I can't believe people like him are here!" She was having to shriek right into Laura's ear.

There were bouncers by the ropes as well now, huge great men with shaven heads. They couldn't even get close enough to linger nearby.

Susie said something that Laura could only just make out about "not being groupies anyway" and they continued to the bar.

As they waited to be served, a skinny, dark haired man started talking to Charlotte. She was hemmed in by him, the bar and the people behind her, so she spoke back to him. At one point Laura saw her laugh.

They took their drinks - Zio Giorgio once again unknowingly obliging - and suddenly Charlotte was pulling them across the room. Having no clue what she was up to they followed, and then in a blur the VIP rope was suddenly lifted and they were in the VIP section.

"Who is that?" Laura asked Susie, fearing she would be expected to know.

Susie shrugged. "No clue."

Laura found herself sitting on a velvet covered seat with Susie squashed up against her left side and some other man, who knew Charlotte's skinny man, on her right.

"This is Tony," Charlotte said to them, practically in a yell.

Tony introduced them to some of the other people there. All the girls seemed to have bleached hair and the same style of heavy make up. Laura forgot everyone's names even as soon as she heard them.

Susie was getting the evil eye from one of them, Laura suspected they had taken their seats.

"You from round here?" one of them asked.

Laura was still dying to know who these people were to have got in the VIP area. She recognised the popstar a couple of tables away but none of the other people around.

"No, are you?"

"She's with him." The blonde, who had black roots and wore a white lycra top and black skirt, indicated her friend and one of the men. The other girl was also blonde with a perm and huge hoop earrings, and the man didn't look familiar or famous at all to Laura.

There was a cheer as someone arrived with a champagne bucket. It frothed out everywhere when the cork was popped, then was sloshed into whatever glasses people were holding. Loads of it got split everywhere.

Laura assumed it would be some kind of fake bubbly but when she got a closer look at the bottle she saw it was the real deal. Thank God they weren't putting this onto Zio Giorgio's card, the price would be unearthly. Someone handed her a glass and she sipped it out of politeness. She was trying to watch her alcohol consumption.

The man next to Laura started trying to chat her up. She had a feeling he might have been called Andy but truly couldn't remember. His hair was dark and styled with gel and he had a black t-shirt under a leather jacket.

"So you like our music?" he asked.

Should she lie? If she said "yes" then he might ask which song, and then she would be stuck. If only Susie was sitting in her place.

"Yes, it's great," she said. She would have to bluff this through.

He started telling her about some gig they had played in Germany in a European tour they had just come back from. Laura was earnestly listening for some kind of clues to figure out who they were.

They were interrupted briefly when one of his presumed bandmates leant over to ask him something, and Laura turned to Susie. "Who?" she mouthed.

Susie whispered the name to her. Or rather semi yelled it into Laura's hair, not wanting the other girls to realise what she was saying.

Oh god, they were really famous. Nearly as much so as the popstar she had recognised. The lead singer wasn't there though, and Laura never really noticed other band members so much. It was the frontmen that everyone remembered and pinned up on their walls. But at least she could now talk coherently about some of their music.

They got very little exposure to popular culture at Francis Hall except in the holidays, and even that was mainly via magazines. Top of the Pops fell during evening prep so they never got to see it except in the holidays. Laura's home in Cornwall was also hours away from London so she didn't get to go to concerts regularly like London girls presumably did.

She managed to corner Charlotte in the restroom. Charlotte was applying more lipstick and trying to fix the make up that had smudged under her eyes. Laura thought it looked good that way: softer and more blended. "What's going on? You can't like him, surely?"

"He's really funny," Charlotte said. "He knows all this stuff about everyone."

"Everyone?"

"The band. Other famous people. It's fascinating." Charlotte was on a high.

Laura looked directly at her. "How drunk are you?"

"Really not that much. He's not even drinking. There's some party afterwards, he says we should all come," Charlotte told her. She was lit up that night. She looked practically like a starlet herself in the little black dress with her long blonde hair and model figure.

Given they had planned to stay up until dawn anyway, having nowhere to go that night, it made as much sense as anything. But Laura felt a bit out of her depth.

"They all seem to know one another. We don't know any of them."

"It doesn't matter. If we absolutely hate it we can just leave. Find an all night café and just hang out or something."

"I guess so." Laura was curious about what such a party might be like. Probably not very enjoyable unless one was absolutely wasted, and she couldn't risk that.

14. The party

They were actually crammed into a black limo when leaving the nightclub. No one seemed fazed by it but Laura was initially impressed. Until she got inside and thought how tacky it was: black mirrors and quilted walls and cigarette burns all over the the seats.

It was a crush of limbs and bodies and hair, sticky with spray, that kept getting brushed into Laura's face by one of the groupie-looking girls. She was relieved when they finally arrived, which didn't take long due to minimal traffic at the late hour.

The party was already in full swing in some huge and grand looking house in west London that was already trashed inside. Laura saw the blond popstar from the club already there, sitting on a sofa surrounded by another group of girls. He looked completely out of it.

That was the one thing that shocked her. Laura had never really come across hard drugs before, except for some parties in Cornwall where there might be a joint passed around. Usually nicked from someone's hippy parents.

Here she actually saw people openly taking substances - cocaine, she assumed it was. She felt like the world's biggest prude when someone offered her some and she turned it down. Charlotte had disappeared altogether and Susie was half draped over some guy who looked a bit like Darius. He wasn't one of the band, at least.

A girl next to her asked her for a cigarette lighter but Laura didn't have one. "I should quit," the girl said. She turned to someone on the other side of her and lit her cigarette from theirs. "Thanks babe." She turned back to Laura.

"So who do you know here?" Her tone was friendly not hostile, which made a nice change. She had lots of dark, wavy hair and a nose stud.

"No one really. We just got asked along at the last moment," Laura said.

The girl offered Laura a cigarette but Laura declined, once again feeling like a square. "I have to work tomorrow, I'll be so wrecked," the girl said.

"Where do you work?"

"Kings Road."

Laura had meant what kind of job, but she assumed from this answer that it was probably a shop. She wondered how old the girl was since she didn't look much older than them, and whether she lived with her family or had her own flat.

She didn't have to ask because the girl had started going on a bit of a rant about her sister and the flat they shared, and some disagreement over "stuff" being left about. Laura wasn't sure whether it was her stuff or her sister's because she was only half listening. She was getting increasingly worried about where Charlotte was as she hadn't seen her for a while now.

The girl nattered on and Laura thought how amazing it must be to have that kind of freedom. Your own place: getting to decide what you did and when. Never having to check in with anyone or ask permission to go places. Unlike all the sneaking around they did.

It had never really bothered her before she met Mr Rydell. Rules hadn't been a problem until then, they were just part of the fabric and boundaries of school life. She hadn't needed to test them before. Now they were this endless, frustrating obstacle in her way.

She wished he were there. She was tired and the thought of just being in his arms, falling into bed with him, was better than this party even if there were famous people here.

* * *

Susie had started getting itchy feet almost as soon as they had got to the party. It wasn't that she was bored, more that she felt unchallenged. She had achieved all her goals that night in terms of clubbing and getting into the scene.

Drugs held no interest for her. Alcohol was no novelty either, given her family owned vineyards. There weren't even any guys around she was particularly attracted to. She was still seeing Darius but it wasn't really exclusive, neither of them were that committed. They got on like a house on fire when they were together, but by mutual understanding it was out of sight, out of mind when they were apart.

Susie had just managed to extricate herself from conversation with some hands-wandering creep who was falling all over the place when one of the endless fake blonde groupie types bumped into her.

The girl swore at her. "Watch where you're going." She was slurring and aggressive, clearly off her face.

Susie recognised her as one of the girls who had been hanging over the popstar earlier. She clearly hadn't got anywhere with him. She was about to move to the other room when the girl grabbed her arm and started yelling at her, clearly spoiling for a fight. Given the girl's state Susie was fairly certain she wouldn't represent much of a challenge, but she didn't want to go back to Francis Hall with a black eye.

She pushed the girl backwards in a swift move and made an even quicker exit.

As she passed the stairs she saw two other girls she hadn't met sitting there, smoking and bitching. Susie realised they were talking about Charlotte, who could be seen through an open doorway in an adjacent room. They were sneering at her and slagging her off for allegedly "throwing herself" at the bass player.

They were just drunk and jealous and Susie should have ignored it but she felt that the gauntlet had been thrown down.

"That's actually my friend you're slagging off. You might want to shut your mouths." Then she walked off, leaving them open mouthed.

There was only one thing she could do get back at them even more, and to satisfy her own sense of ennui. To see if she could score with the prize of the night: the popstar.

He was still on the sofa in the main living room. Susie walked up there, said "excuse me" to one of the crowd around him, and pushed her way through to forcibly sit next to him. She had discovered from past experience that doing something outrageously bold usually confounded people and left a clear path.

After all, what was the worst that could happen? Possibly she might get thrown out. But the prospect didn't overly concern her. She didn't know these people nor care what they thought about her either.

The popstar turned to look at her. He looked nowhere near as attractive as in the posters of him, Susie thought. There were fine lines around the corners of his eyes, his face was puffy and his pupils were dilated to the size of dinner plates.

"I'm Susie," she said, and smiled. She had inherited Zia Viola's devastating combination of charm and wickedness.

Dark-haired and fresher faced, Susie stood out among the crowd of interchangeable, heavily made-up blondes. She was also younger than many of them. As high as he was, this didn't escape his notice.

"Did Marco invite you?" he asked.

Susie had no idea who Marco was. "No, I gatecrashed."

He laughed. Susie felt the click. They connected, she had his attention.

"Should I throw you out?"

"Probably."

She was running on adrenalin now. Even for Susie, this was big game.

He stared at her for a moment, his eyes not quite focusing. Abruptly he stood up. "I've got to take a piss."

Susie was disconcerted, but he held out his hand. "You coming?"

She supposed she was. She followed him, a crowd of savage eyes on her back. Was he actually going to the bathroom? Was he into something weird? Susie had no idea but she decided to ride with it.

He pushed people out of the way from the bathroom, or rather one of the bathrooms as a house this large would clearly have several. He shut the door and actually took a leak, with Susie standing behind him not knowing if she was supposed to look away or not. Being Susie she didn't really care, she was more curious than offended.

He zipped up, didn't bother to flush or wash his hands or even look in the mirror. "Let's go upstairs."

Upstairs was a bedroom. A fairly regular looking one, not some debauched den of black sheets and ceiling mirrors. There were a couple of people sitting on the floor, leaning against the bed smoking a joint. He kicked them out and they didn't protest.

About the only thing that suggested the music industry was a guitar leaning against the wall. Beyond that it was a bit of a mess, the bedclothes half pulled back, playing cards strewn on a table. Not many clothes or personal effects. It wasn't clear if this was his room or a spare room.

He sat on the bed and offered her a joint. Susie only took half a drag as she wanted to keep her wits about her. He reclined and continued to smoke, not saying anything. Susie wondered if he was expecting her to take the initiative and service him while he lay there like his groupies presumably did. Which she herself had no intention of doing.

Eventually he spoke. "Fucking Marco."

"Who's Marco?" Susie asked.

"My manager."

Then without warning he rolled over and kissed her. His mouth was dry and smoky and Susie wished he taken a swig of drink first. In her head she was marvelling at how this would be a dream for thousands of girls, and how mundane it was in reality.

* * *

Laura hadn't seen Charlotte for hours and now Susie had disappeared. Several people had tried to chat her up but she had managed to excuse herself. There was no real pressure. Girls outnumbered guys so there was plenty of prey.

She figured she may as well go and look for her friends. She wandered through various rooms feeling a bit out of place. Laura knew she didn't look out of place but inside it was a different story.

She opened a bathroom door by accident and saw one of the band members from the nightclub sprawled out over the floor. There was a girl next to him trying to scrape up a trace of white powder from the floor tiles, using a credit card. Laura left them well alone.

After going upstairs and trying a couple of rooms she finally found Susie. She was lying on the bed next to the half-passed-out popstar. Susie rolled her eyes and greeted her.

The popstar looked Laura up and down through half-closed eyes, his gaze appreciative. He managed to get to his feet. "Excuse me." He left though another door in the room, not bothering to close it behind him. Laura could see it was the ensuite. They heard the seat go up and the sound of water and the two girls looked at one another and suppressed laughter.

"What are you up to?" Laura asked Susie.

"Not much. He's too coked up and stoned to do anything. He kissed me and then he rolled over and looked like he was going to fall asleep."

"Did you take anything?"

"One drag of his joint, that's pretty much all," Susie told her. "I'm nearly back to being stone cold sober. He didn't even bring any alcohol."

"This is so weird."

"I know. No one would believe us if we told them."

"If they did they'd expel us," Laura said.

Their conversation was interrupted by the popstar staggering back from the bathroom while zipping up his flies.

Susie and Laura caught one another's eyes again. They were both trying not to laugh.

"Where's Marco?"

"In the garden."

He looked confused at Susie's answer but left the room through the main door.

Susie lay back on the bed and yawned. "God I'm exhausted. I wonder if we could sleep here?"

"Have you seen Charlotte anywhere?" Laura asked.

"Not for ages. We should probably go and find her."

They found Charlotte in a kind of conservatory at the back of the house, sitting in a circle with the bassist and other people they didn't recognise. The room reeked of cannabis. Charlotte was completely out of it but she seemed safe enough.

Susie and Laura decided to leave her there and go back upstairs and crash. They had meant to stay up all night but their enthusiasm for that was waning.

They went back to the previous bedroom which was still empty. "What if he comes back?" Laura asked, referring to the popstar.

"He's probably got some other girl all over him already. We'll be fine."

* * *

Wired with adrenalin and the intensity of the night, and in a strange bed in a strange house, Laura had worried that she wouldn't be able to sleep. But once she lay down her whole body felt heavy, her head ringing, and oblivion came.

Hours later when she woke she could barely remember how she had got there. She was hungover, her mouth was so dry and uncomfortable that despite still feeling too exhausted to move she went to swill her mouth with water from the basin.

She hated waking up in the same clothes from the night before but there wasn't a lot she could do about it. She also longed for a shower. It struck her that their hair must stink of cigarette smoke and other substances. How on earth could they arrive back at Francis Hall in such a state?

Susie was still asleep on the bed so Laura nudged her.

"It's morning, I think."

Susie groaned. "What time? Let's get out of here."

They found Charlotte who was sleeping on a sofa with the bass player. Someone had thrown a blanket over them.

"We've got to go," Susie told her.

They managed to get Charlotte to her feet - to Laura's relief, Charlotte was still fully clothed - during which time the bass player woke. Then a biro had to be found so Charlotte could write her number on his arm at his request. Eventually they got her away, Laura practically pulling her by the arm.

"What's the rush?" the bassist said.

"Train to catch."

Tottering down the road to find a tube station in their heels, revived by the freezing morning air, it felt like they owned the world. Everything had come off. It had been a wilder, weirder night than they could have imagined.

Charlotte even had a brainwave about the problem of the cigarette odour. "We'll get some dry shampoo from Boots."

It turned out to be horrible, powdery stuff that left their hair feeling even more rank and dirty than before, but it managed to mask the smell of stale cigarettes. Liberal amounts of body spray freshened everything else up enough to put their school uniforms back on.

Their nightclub outfits were sealed in plastic bags, they could be dry-cleaned at half term. Fortunately their school coats had avoided the worst of it, having been in the nightclub's cloakroom, and would hopefully get an airing on the train journey back.

Laura felt that they had almost been too lucky with everything working out so well.

"It's not luck, it's planning," Susie said.

15. Back at school

The bond between the three of them was stronger than ever after they returned to school, though they tried to include Margery. She was disbelieving at first and envious, being a fan of the star that Susie had briefly kissed.

"You'd be disappointed if you met him in the flesh," Susie told her. "He was quite seedy."

Margery was bewildered as to how Susie had still kissed him if this was so, but said nothing. She was even more shocked to hear about the woman from the modelling agency approaching Charlotte.

"There's no way you could do that, your father would go mad."

Nonetheless Margery was excited for Charlotte. They all were. It was like a dream come true, having someone actually pick you out in the street like that.

"You could go up at half term maybe," Laura suggested. "Just see what she has to say."

Charlotte was sitting on her bed in their dorm, wrapped up in a dressing gown with her hair in a towel after finally washing the previous night out of it. She tried to sound casual about it. "I'll see." She had carefully put Barbara's card in her drawer and copied the number to her diary, so the others knew she was taken with the idea.

Susie was particularly satisfied with the London outing. She had achieved what she had set out to do and more. But she wasn't someone who needed to boast about her feats, which frustrated the others.

"Can you imagine the look on Teresa Hubert's face if she knew who you'd snogged?" Charlotte said. She was dying to brag on Susie's behalf.

"There's no point, it's lose-lose. Either people won't believe us and we'll just look sad, or word will really get about and we'll be in huge trouble," Susie said. Saying this she idly wondered how such a thing could be proved. Photos, possibly. Or actually producing the man in question and parading him around Francis Hall. She laughed out loud thinking about this.

"What's so funny?" Margery asked.

"I was just imagining people's reactions if he turned up here and took a tour of the school," Susie said. In fact, just producing Ferdinando and Massimo would be reasonably sensational, they were both so good looking. She must think about it. Susie had no interest in showing off or trying to impress people with her connections, but she liked the idea of stirring things up.

"Imagine if he called you," Margery said.

"He doesn't have my number, and really, he's not my type."

"He's so famous though," Margery said. She had never met anyone famous and couldn't understand why Susie wasn't more excited. She was secretly hoping that there might be some way she could get his autograph.

"No more than that guy that Charlotte scored. Or his band, anyway. What phone number did you give him by the way?"

Charlotte looked embarrassed. "I meant to give him a fake number but I was so out of it."

"So what did you write down?" Laura asked.

It turned out that Charlotte had actually written down the number at Michaelmas house. Susie was delighted. "I hope he calls. And that Gi-Gi answers. Good luck pretending he's your cousin or whatever."

They deliberately kept Charlotte's modelling approach hush-hush. It was the kind of thing that sounded boastful no matter how you mentioned it, and Charlotte didn't want anyone to know. After all, it was only a business card so far.

* * *

Teresa Hubert could tell something was up. Her sworn enemies were thicker than thieves and even more pleased with themselves than ever. This infuriated her. If they saw her approach they occasionally did the Italian thing but she was increasingly convinced that Charlotte was faking it. Something Charlotte had said in response to Susie the other day sounded suspiciously similar to some lines of Vergil they'd had to memorise for Mr Tyrell's Latin homework.

It would be great to catch them out in some way, but that would require finding someone who knew Italian and Teresa couldn't think of anyone.

She had also noticed how well they all got on with Tom Hollier and in particular Susie's behaviour towards him. She was alternately outrageously rude or outrageously suggestive. Teresa supposed that Susie was in his Geography class but it still couldn't explain the level of familiarity she displayed.

Was something going on between them? It was surely an absurd thought, but Teresa couldn't help thinking it.

Then there was the fact that Susie and the others had signed up for Orienteering Club which seemed very odd to Teresa. Something was behind that, for sure. It was her mission to get to the bottom of it.

"You must have been sad to miss out on orienteering last weekend," she said to Laura when they were both in the common room at Michaelmas House. Orienteering Club had been cancelled for the exeat.

Laura, who was making a cup of tea, was at first confused by the question and frowned. Then it rapidly dawned on her that Teresa was digging once again. For what though, Laura had no idea.

"Not really, not in this weather," she said.

Teresa decided to be more direct.

"I was surprised to see you all joining Orienteering Club. I wouldn't have thought that would be your style."

"Wouldn't you?" Laura's tone was infuriatingly polite.

"Perhaps it's due to Tom Hollier. He's very handsome, isn't he? I'm sure Susie has noticed. What with being in his Geography class."

Laura wished the kettle would hurry up and boil so she could escape Teresa.

"As I'm sure you have too," Teresa continued, "given your own special relationship with another member of staff."

Laura looked at Teresa. She found herself wondering why Teresa continued to be so nasty.

"What did you do for half term?" she asked, changing the subject.

Teresa was taken aback. "Half term? What's that got to do with anything?"

Laura shrugged. "Nothing really." Hallelujah, the kettle had finally started to make its loud angry boiling sound. The thermostat was faulty so it didn't always switch itself off. She quickly started pouring water into a mug with a teabag in it.

"We were talking about you, weren't we, and what you did or didn't get up to with Mr Rydell last term?" Teresa was nothing if not persistent.

"Were we?" Laura said, managing to maintain her polite tone. "Perhaps you were."

Her tea finished she made a swift exit out of the room, up the stairs and to the sanctuary of the dorm.

* * *

"Teresa really seems to be on our case this term," Laura told the others once she was safely back in the dorm.

"Nothing new there." Charlotte was unconcerned.

"She's being weird though. It's as though she's desperate to find stuff out. More than usual," Laura said.

Charlotte was putting on a face mask. She had become paranoid about getting spots in case anything did happen with Barbara Banks and the modelling agency. She still hadn't completely decided whether she would call them or not.

Susie was laughing at the results. "You look like a muddy green gargoyle," she said. "Honestly those things never work. If you want to avoid spots you have to stop eating sweets and chocolate, and drink masses of water."

Charlotte, who loved chocolate and had a very healthy appetite due to all the exercise she did, preferred trying the face mask. "It's got minerals in it," she said.

"Coal has minerals in it."

"Coal is a mineral," Margery pointed out.

Laura squeezed out some of the leftover mask onto her fingers. "It feels like runny clay." She looked at the sachet. "It is clay. We could probably nick some from the art room and make it ourselves."

"You should put it on half your face," Susie suggested, "and see if in a week's time one side is any different to the other."

"Half Lancôme, half Mr Lanaway," Laura said, referring to the art master.

Charlotte looked disgusted. "That sounds absolutely foul and like something quite different."

Susie laughed. "That's just your dirty mind. Besides, they actually say it's good for the skin." She grinned again as Charlotte grimaced.

"What's good for the skin?" Margery asked, looking confused. "Clay?"

It was one of those moments when explaining the joke was simply too awkward. Laura felt sorry for Margery because she didn't want her to feel humiliated at not getting it or left out as she was the one with least experience in these things. "Supposedly, but probably not art room clay," she said and changed the subject to a horrendous essay topic that Mr Peters had given them.

Charlotte, whose mask had now dried and cracked her face into wrinkles like someone's alien grandmother, complained to Susie. "If only you could see your way to sweeten him up maybe he'd be easier on us this term."

Margery looked shocked even though Charlotte was joking but Susie looked pensive.

"If I get really bored, I mean really super bored, then I might try winding him up. But for now there are other fish to fry."

"I hope you don't mean Mr Hollier," Margery said. Susie's behaviour towards him had unsettled her.

Once again Susie grinned, her eyes glinting with fun and her teeth brilliantly white. "Not that sort of fish, Margie. Charlotte's modelling career for a start. As well as some other plans I have."

This struck terror into the heart of Margery so she said no more. Laura and Charlotte also exchanged a glance. They had thought that escapades were over for the term, but you never knew what to expect with Susie.

16. Valentine's Day

Laura was by the staff room, trying to put an essay into the history teacher's pigeon hole. The problem was that they weren't in alphabetical order and the positions seemed to change almost every term. This, combined with the names being typed in tiny letters, resulted in her struggling to find it.

"Posting valentines?"

It was Mr Hollier, who was on his way to the staff room.

Laura was momentarily confused. "No, I was just…"

"Don't worry, I was just joking." He smiled at her. "It is the fourteenth of February."

How could she forget? How could any of them forget? There had been an intense flurry of desperation that morning with people waiting for the first post, and some lucky girls getting bouquets and looking smug about it.

For her part Laura wasn't really expecting anything. The post remained a risk and she was seeing Mr Rydell at half term anyway. Just days away now. She couldn't wait.

Tom Hollier had stopped at his pigeonhole where he drew out a pile of papers. A couple fluttered down and Laura could see that they were valentines. She hid a smile and tried to pretend she hadn't seen, but it was obvious.

Susie would have been merciless in teasing him but Laura could see that he was embarrassed.

"At least you haven't been forgotten," she said.

He gathered his mail together. There were at least half a dozen envelopes and folded papers that looked likely to be love notes, as well as the two he had picked up. "This would be a record for me" he said, looking rueful.

She doubted that, unless he had been teaching at a boys' school before.

"Perhaps they're all from the Headmistress," Laura said, trying to make light of it.

"I'll have to check her handwriting."

Laura wondered how many valentines would have been in the pigeonhole labelled Mr Rydell - now pasted over with Frau Beinhof - if had still been at the school. She also wondered how she would have felt about him getting loads. It was certain that he would have received some: even portly Mr Poynter the History teacher and pale Mr Lanaway in Art got them.

Admittedly they were more for fun in Mr Lanaway's case. Laura couldn't imagine anyone seriously having a crush on the Art master. He was a nice man but his romantic inclinations clearly lay in another direction.

Even Mr Tyrrell had received a valentine last year. Obviously a joke from some of the sixth form students, it had reportedly contained explicit verses from Catullus and caused Mr Tyrrell to turn beet red and leave the classroom.

At that moment Mr Peters came by, brisk with his own self-importance. His glance passed over the fat bundle that Tom Hollier was holding. His own pigeonhole appeared to contain a single sheet of paper that looked like a memorandum, certainly no cards or billets-doux.

His lips tightened and he swept past them without even bothering to retrieve it.

Laura caught Mr Hollier's eye. They were both trying not to laugh.

"Perhaps he picked his up earlier," Laura said.

"I'll donate him some of mine."

* * *

Laura saw Tom Hollier again at the end of the day because she had to pick up a form for an orienteering event that her parents needed to sign over half term.

There were flowers in his room - several bunches - as well as gifts and cards that he had tried to stack unobtrusively. He saw her notice them.

"Mrs Grayson has been generous," she said.

"I think she took pity on me."

He handed her a form.

"Did you want me to take ones for the others? Susie and Margery, I mean."

"Thanks, that would be a help. So were you deluged as well?" he asked.

Laura was confused. "Deluged?"

"With valentines."

There had been flowers waiting for her back at Michaelmas House when she had stopped by there after lunch. She hadn't been able to resist waiting until the evening in case Mr Rydell had sent her something. And there they were: a dozen red roses and a dozen white orchids. Easily the most vast, spectacular and expensive bouquet that anyone had received, including the sixth form girls.

Laura had managed to move them to the dorm before they could be widely noticed but unfortunately a couple of girls were also back at the House and saw them. They would be the talk of the school by tomorrow.

"Just flowers." She smiled, thinking of them and the happiness made her radiant. For Laura it was enough that she had received something, that Mr Rydell was thinking of her. Even a single rose would have been just as good.

Tom saw the joy on her face. "I'm afraid these don't inspire quite as much delight." He showed her a crudely drawn Valentine's card. Inside was a comically obscene twist on "Roses are red, Violets are blue" in Susie's distinctive and utterly undisguised handwriting.

Laura couldn't help laughing. "You know she's not serious, don't you?" she said, seeing his consternation at the card.

"I had suspected she wasn't. Hoped, anyway."

"She has a boyfriend at St Duncan's. She just gets a bit cooped up here and likes to joke around." That didn't quite describe Susie's continual attempts to torment Tom Hollier but it was hard to put into words. "If she was really serious, I mean if she had someone in her sights, she'd be a lot more subtle." They wouldn't know what had hit them, Laura thought.

"That's something of a relief. So were your flowers another example of the gallantry of St Duncan's?"

"No. He's not..." she was about to say "not at school" but that might raise awkward questions "...at St Duncan's."

"A boy back home?"

"Something like that." It was safest if people thought this. She could only imagine the Geography teacher's reaction if she told him the truth.

At least he understood about Susie. Laura had been worried that Susie might have given him the wrong impression but if he had started to worry, he was now set straight.

* * *

As expected Laura's flowers caused something of a sensation at Michaelmas House later that evening. Enough word had spread that people kept coming to their dorm for a viewing. Grace Grant, who was fairly certain she knew the sender, made no comment and kept out of the way. It was better if these things blew over quickly.

At least Laura wasn't the kind of girl to court attention. She had been genuinely embarrassed by the level of interest in the flowers. Grace Grant wondered at the sense of the former German teacher - if indeed her hunch was right - at sending such an ostentatious arrangement. They must have cost a fortune.

Not to mention the difficulty of finding vases for them. Laura had ended up having to use a bucket from the janitor's closet.

"I feel awful putting them in a plastic bucket," she said.

"I shouldn't worry, that's what florists keep flowers in. They're so enormous you can hardly see it anyway," Susie told her. "They'd topple most vases over and then we'd have glass everywhere."

Teresa was both suspicious and enraged with jealousy. A couple of sixth formers had jokingly referred to Laura as "flower girl" and Teresa and her henchwomen adopted this epithet with the nastiest sarcasm possible. Until Susie started called Teresa "no-flower girl" which rapidly shut her up.

"I shouldn't be surprised if she sent them to herself," Teresa was heard to mutter. She had tried peeking to see if there was a card but Laura had wisely removed this and hidden it away. It was written by the florist anyway, and just said: "All my love, always."

So it was reasonably safe even if other people did see it. Had Mr Rydell used a German quote it would have been a huge giveaway.

Charlotte had a card and chocolates that were obviously from Julian. It gave her a mild twinge of guilt over the Italian guy as she feared that Julian might be more attached than she was. She still hadn't told Julian about the modelling thing because she couldn't think of a way to phrase it in a letter that didn't sound vain or boastful.

"It really doesn't sound like you're boasting," Laura said. "It's just what happened. But by all means wait until you've seen them again before mentioning it."

Susie had received a black orchid that Margery thought was funereal. "It looks more creepy than a romantic gesture," she said.

"It's a little joke we have, so I know it's from Darius," she told Margery. She didn't expound what the joke was. There was no card from Darius, but Susie had received a couple of others in the post as well as one slipped into her locker.

From the reek of aftershave they all guessed it was from Mr Peters. Featuring a watercolour of roses, it looked like the kind of card you would buy your grandmother for her eightieth birthday. It contained one of Shakespeare's sonnets, photocopied from a book and then cut out and glued inside the card.

"I remember that one," Laura said. "I think it's about Shakespeare's penis."

"Which bit?" Charlotte was avid to see.

Susie quoted a couple of lines: "Flesh stays no farther reason, but rising at thy name doth point out thee."

"That's the bit," Laura said. "He obviously hasn't given up then."

"I'm sure it's not the only one he sent," Susie said, displaying it on her bedside table. "It wouldn't surprise me if half the sixth form got a choice quote or two."

"You can't put it there!" Charlotte was horrified. "What if someone sees?"

"Besides it really is creepy," Laura agreed. Everything about it was creepy.

But Susie seemed greatly entertained by it. "If I leave it here, Matron will see it, and doubtless smell it. If he has given a few dozen out to other girls, she may well see a few of those as well and the plot will thicken."

"What plot?" Margery asked.

"Any plot you like. A catfight between all the Valentine recipients for the affections of Mr Peters."

Margery didn't understand how Susie could be so flippant about something so abhorrent and wrong. "I think Julian's Valentine was the nicest. Not that your roses weren't beautiful," she said to Laura, "but a card and chocolates seems the most sensible and appropriate thing to send."

Charlotte rolled her eyes. "I'm not sure I'm particularly thrilled at having this year's most sensible Valentine."

"You know what I mean. It shows the most judgement and discretion," Margery said.

"Except we're not living in the page of a Victorian novel," Charlotte said. She was regretting the fact that Julian hadn't sent flowers. Still, at least you could eat chocolates and dinner that evening had been beyond inedible.

17. Half term

Charlotte had finally plucked up the courage to ring Barbara Banks, the woman from the modelling agency. The others accompanied her, with Susie ready to play Cyrano de Bergerac and prompt Charlotte if she lost her nerve and her words.

She got through to a receptionist. "Could I speak with Barbara Banks, please?"

"Is she expecting your call?"

"No, well, she gave me her business card and told me to call her," Charlotte said. "She didn't specify when."

"So you're not on our books currently?"

"No."

"Okay." Charlotte could hear the receptionist pressing buttons and an engaged tone in the back ground. "She's on the other line now. Can you hold? No - wait - I think she's coming clear."

Charlotte was suddenly connected with Barbara.

"Hello, my name is Charlotte Bevan. You gave me your card in Oxford Street and asked me to call you."

There was a pause. "Tall girl, blonde?" Barbara also named the shoe shop they had encountered her in.

"Yes, that's the one. I am sorry for bumping into you," Charlotte said.

"That's quite alright. We may both be thanking our lucky stars for that fall one day. When can you come in for a chat?"

"The thing is I'm at school. Boarding school. It's half term in a couple of weeks though."

"That's fine. What about the Monday. Can you bring a parent or guardian with you?"

No way in hell. "I'm not sure..."

"It's alright if not, we can sort that out later depending how we go."

The time, date and location were fixed. There was no going back.

Except Charlotte had no idea how she was going to get there nor what to tell her parents.

Laura would have loved to have helped but she was absolutely committed to seeing her parents in Cornwall at the start of the week, so she could spend the rest of it with Mr Rydell.

Susie had been summoned to stay with her parents as they were actually in England that week, and she had spent practically all of the Christmas break with her Italian aunt and uncle.

"It could have been worse," she told them. "At least I wasn't condemned to the house of Aunt Morgan and Uncle Tim." These were her father's sister and brother-in-law, who lived about an hour away from the school, and acted as guardians for Susie when her parents were overseas. Susie was in fact looking forward to seeing her parents, her mother in particular. She had plenty of gossip from Zia Viola to pick over with her.

Help came from a surprising source. Margery offered to have Charlotte stay with her. "I'll get my father to write to yours, and we can get the train up to London if you like."

"Oh that would be so sweet of you, Margery. I just hope my parents agree."

"There's some French play my father wanted to take me to. I'll have him mention that, then maybe your father will think it's an educational trip."

It was all settled. How much easier their lives would be without all this subterfuge and sneaking around, Laura thought. Susie thrived on it but Laura herself was tiring of it all.

* * *

Charlotte found that she was glad to have Margery's company to her appointment in London. They hadn't spent so much time together this school year, what with Susie and her escapades, their boyfriends at St Duncan's and the Italian trip. Margery was always too shy to want to participate but they had all missed her. It was difficult, getting out of step with a close friend.

As they travelled in on the train, talking about this and that, Charlotte adjusted her perceptions. It wasn't so much that they had left Margery behind and become more sophisticated while she remained a studious schoolgirl. It was simply that for now, Margery had chosen to take a different path. Her studies had always been important to her and she had her heart set on a particular university and was putting everything into achieving that. It was no different from Charlotte's hockey, really. Just a different interest and a different goal.

Charlotte found she could still talk easily with Margery about Julian and boys and things. Even if Margery lacked personal experience she still had perspective and even wisdom.

She also displayed more curiosity than Charlotte had expected, she had got the impression before that Margery wasn't really interested in talking about boyfriends and things.

"What was it like, seeing Mr Rydell and Laura together in Italy? Was it strange?" Margery asked her.

Charlotte had to think about this for a moment. "Yes it was, at times. Some of the time it was like she was there with a teacher, and it was all wrong and forbidden, and I kept expecting Mrs Grayson to jump out from behind a bush. Then the rest of the time it just seemed really normal. Just like she had an older boyfriend."

"What's he like, out of school?"

"Honestly? He really is quite amazing. I mean I can see why she's so mad about him. He's so good looking and he knows stuff and he was the only one of us who could talk with Susie's uncle. And he's so in love with her, you can just see it all the time," Charlotte told her.

"How do you mean?"

"It's like he really cares for her, he's sort of protective. I can't really describe it. But in a good way. They're really good together, Margery, honestly. I know you've had your doubts but they just seemed right, as a couple. Laura seemed older maybe. But not in a bad way. Like she was more peaceful, calmer."

Charlotte was increasingly less calm herself as they approached the location of the modelling agency. They had to get a tube from the main train station and she was anxious about how she looked and what she should say.

Margery was surprised to find Charlotte so invested in the idea of modelling.

"It's just that if this happened I could maybe start making my own money. And then..." Charlotte didn't need to finish. Having her own money simply meant freedom. A wealthy father was meaningless when he was so controlling with the purse strings. Thank god he hadn't so far objected to her hockey, as his focus was usually on her schooling.

"Wouldn't you need your parents' permission though."

"Probably." Charlotte's hope was that Barbara could somehow pull a rabbit out of a hat. But she was getting ahead of herself. There was every chance that Barbara would take a second look at her and recoil with shock and disappointment.

According to Susie's guidance, Charlotte had worn quite normal clothes - just jeans and a top - and minimal make up. "You don't want to slather yourself," Susie told her. "They do all that for you, if they need. Most models go pretty much bare faced to everything especially castings."

They wondered how Susie knew all this.

"My cousin models, remember? I've been back stage with him in Milan and stuff. Just leave your hair loose, don't put tonnes of lipstick on or anything."

The agency had a very futuristic, modern reception. It was all white and dove grey with a few objects in bright orange and blue. There were framed magazine covers and photos on the wall, presumably of models the agency represented. Several of them were quite famous. Charlotte was starting to lose her nerve.

The receptionist had given her a clipboard and a form to fill out while she waited for Barbara. There was another girl waiting as well, a very thin mousy looking girl with a wide mouth, apparently accompanied by her mother.

"I can't put my home address here, what if they write and my father opens it?" Charlotte said.

"You can hardly put Francis Hall down. Or maybe you could, after all they're not to know that Michaelmas House is a boarding school house and not just someone's home. In fact why not just use its street address - 17 Hargate Road - that's perfect."

Charlotte thanked Margery for her ingenuity. "But what about the phone number?"

"You'll just have to put the one in the hall for now."

Other details were easier to fill out, such as date of birth, height and weight. Medical conditions: none.

Finally Charlotte was ushered down a corridor and into a dazzlingly light office where Barbara rose from behind the desk to greet her. "Hello Charlotte, thanks for coming." She looked her up and down. "Just turn around". Charlotte did so. "Great, I thought I remembered you pretty well. Let's have a quick chat and take a few shots when Yves is ready."

She invited Charlotte to sit down in a sofa in the corner of the room and sat across from her in an arm chair. It was all steel and glass and leather, more stylish than comfortable. Charlotte tried not to feel intimidated at all the famous faces around her.

"So you're at boarding school, planning to do A-levels?" Charlotte nodded. "Always wise. Most of our younger models are restricted to holidays and weekends. How do your parents feel about this."

Charlotte's face said it all.

"They don't know? They're like that, are they? I'm afraid we will need their permission if you want to sign with us, but we can cross that bridge later."

She gave Charlotte a brief remit of the agency, mentioning some of the talent on their books. "Those girls of course represent only a very tiny percentage of models. For most it's part time work, often irregular, and a very short career. When you do work, you will be well paid, but there are no guarantees."

The phone on her desk beeped and Barbara picked it up. "Thanks Daisy. Yves is ready," she told Charlotte. "You'll be fine as you are, this is just to give us an idea."

A woman, who turned out to be Daisy, came in and Charlotte was handed over to her. She said goodbye to Barbara and it was the last she saw of her on that occasion.

Charlotte had initially thought that Barbara said "Eve" but later discovered the photographer was Yves, a man. French, with tousled hair and heavy lidded eyes that made him look languid. When it came to his craft he as a sharp as a tack, barking directions at an assistant one moment then instantly switching to charm, trying to set Charlotte at her ease and get what he wanted.

She felt the exploratory sense of the photo session. He was starting from scratch, he was trying to see what was there. It was disconcerting: she ended up feeling removed from her own body and skin, as though it was just something for Yves and her to manipulate and arrange. Her mind was disconnected from herself.

Yves was also very attractive. Charlotte wasn't so naive to think that the flattering phrases he reeled off meant anything, they were purely to relax her. He must photograph dozens of beautiful women every week. Still, it was nice posing for him. For a short time she was the complete centre of attention and it gave her a strange and lovely glow inside.

18. Cornwall

Cornwall was grey and freezing in February. Elsewhere the winter weather seemed to matter less. But here, bordered by the sea and sand, by the beaches and rocky coves where people flocked in summer, it seemed bitterly bleak.

Inside her home it was warm, and it was lovely being with her family again. That was the thing with boarding school, you became distanced. Laura wondered if any of them had really bargained for it: the effects of the separation.

Back with her parents and brother, the family dog and the fat grey cat who hogged the fireside, she could almost convince herself nothing had changed. That there was no breach within this cosy, familiar kinship.

But she knew it was a lie. Being at Francis Hall had first prised a gap there. And Mr Rydell had widened it, beyond all measure.

Laura regretted not being able to tell her mother about him. They had never had secrets before, and she had always relied on her mother's advice. Now she couldn't even breathe a word about the most important thing in her life. She thought her mother probably suspected there was a boy on the scene, and perhaps even felt hurt that Laura wasn't confiding in her.

How could she tell her what had actually happened? That six months ago her entire world had changed, from the moment a pair of dark grey eyes met hers in German class. That even though it was wrong, forbidden, illicit, they couldn't help themselves. That although all reason spoke against it, it felt more right than anything else she had ever known.

Her parents had been thrilled with her report card. Even more so at the suggestion she try for the Upper School scholarship and even Oxbridge when the time came. This assuaged Laura's guilt somewhat, and she also confided some of her friends' news so her mother wouldn't feel completely shut out.

"How exciting for Charlotte," her mother had said, after learning about the modelling opportunity. "She always was a very tall and pretty girl. I wonder how her father will take it?"

It was interesting how Charlotte's mother never seemed to have a voice, Laura thought. But as soon as anyone had met Mr Bevan, extraordinarily strict and controlling as he was, you realised the futility of his wife putting up any resistance. Laura's parents had previously met the Bevans and been quite taken aback by him.

"They don't know," Laura said.

"I imagine they'll have to find out eventually."

Laura poured another cup of tea for them both. "If it all happens and she gets some big contract, he might not mind. Or apparently you can emancipate yourself if you need to, and not need your parents' permission."

"That seems a drastic step to take. And what about school?"

"Oh she's still determined to stay at Francis Hall, whatever happens. Because of hockey more than anything," Laura said.

"And how's Margery?" her mother asked. She had always liked Margery, a polite, sensible girl.

"She's alright. She invited me for next exeat.'"

This wasn't exactly true. Laura would probably be staying with Mr Rydell again for the next exeat, but Margery had offered to be her cover if she needed.

"It's a shame we live so far, I'd love for you to be able to have your friends over more often. We must have some of them to stay over the summer. Particularly that Italian girl who invited you for the New Year. We haven't even met her yet."

"Susie?" Laura wondered what her parents would make of her. "She's only half-Italian. I'll ask her, but I think she and her parents spend a lot of the summer overseas."

* * *

There were only a few Cornwall friends to catch up with, largely because Laura had been separated from the local crowd due to going away to school. There was a girl called Annie whom she still hung out with, they'd once been almost best friends, but every year her life and those of the others seemed to be diverging from Laura's. Many of them planned to quit school early and some already had. Annie wanted to become a beautician. The idea of going to university, even doing A-levels, was alien to her.

They walked shivering along the seafront. So many small shops and cafés were shut at this time of year, only opening up when the first of the tourists started trickling through in late Spring.

Strangely Laura felt on more of an equal footing with Annie this holiday. There had been a time after Annie started getting into boys, long before Laura had, when Laura had felt a bit left behind. Annie had been allowed to get a perm and pierce her navel. She was the girl that all the boys noticed and went after. She always knew about everything from reading her older sisters' magazines and had lost her virginity really early.

Now Laura had caught up with her, at least to some extent. Finally they could talk about sex without it being a one-way conversation. While Laura didn't give Annie the exact details - there was always a concern that rumours might travel in the small community, and reach Laura's parents' ears - she could at least share that she was seeing someone.

"So is he going to come and meet your parents, this man of yours?" Annie asked.

"Not at the moment. He travels a lot," Laura told her.

"You mean they wouldn't approve?"

"You know what parents are like."

But Annie wasn't satisfied with this. "What's he like? Has he got a criminal record or something? Facial tattoos?" She had recently had a butterfly inked on her shoulder which Laura had admired. She could just imagine the apocalypse that would result at Francis Hall if someone came back with a tattoo. She wasn't even aware of any staff members having them.

"Nothing like that. He's just a bit..."

"...married? Don't tell me you're seeing a married guy! Has he got kids?"

Laura was laughing now. "No, no kids, no tattoos. He's not on parole. He's just a bit older than me and I'm not sure how they'll take it."

"Like your dad's age?"

"God no! Just a few years older, not ancient." Laura winced at calling her father ancient, he had only just turned fifty. But for the first time she was glad that he was fifty because if he was as young as Annie's father, who was still in his thirties, he would have been closer to Mr Rydell's age than hers. And that was an unbearable prospect.

"Well good for you. I'm sick of all the talent round here. Or I mean the lack of it. Cornwall is so cut off, I'd love to go up and live in London," Annie said.

"Why don't you?"

"Money. The usual. I'm trying to save up though, for the next couple of years. Then we'll see. I mean they must need beauticians up there as well, mustn't they?"

"More than here, I expect," Laura said. She told Annie about the clubbing expedition and Annie was impressed and envious.

"Your boyfriend didn't mind you clubbing without him?"

"He doesn't know. I mean I'll tell him, I just haven't had a chance yet. It's not easy making phone calls from school." Laura felt anxious about telling him, if truth be told. She knew he hadn't been entirely comfortable with her clubbing in Italy. He would never try to stop her, she knew that, but he minded. Probably for her safety as much as anything.

They went into a café that faced the sea. In the summer you sat outside, but it was far too cold for that. There were some people in there that Annie knew well, and Laura knew a little. One was a boy she had liked one summer holiday. Jake. But he had been going out with someone else then so she had had to nurse her crush in secret.

Looking at him now, she could hardly imagine what she had seen in him. He was just a boy, averagely good looking, with freckles and hair that could do with a cut. He had a chipped front tooth that she had found the height of appeal two years ago.

"Haven't seen you in a while," Jake said to her.

"She's been away. At her posh boarding school," another of them said. He'd acquired a stud below his lip since Laura had last seen him. She had never liked him much, he often seemed to be having a dig at her.

"Leave it off," Annie said.

"You're looking well," Jake said. Even a year ago this would have been the biggest thrill for Laura. Now it made her feel uncomfortable, because the way he was looking at her suggested he was finally interested in her. Which meant that if he made a move she would have to turn him down, and that was always awkward.

"Thanks." She would have said "you too" but didn't want to lead him on.

They ordered Cokes and hot chips, which were shared around. Little packets of salt spilled all over the chipped Formica tables. Laura felt fondly towards the tattiness of the place. At least they hadn't changed it. She never liked coming back from school to find things were different.

"Do you want to go for a walk down the beach later?" Jake asked. There was only one thing that this meant and it wasn't beachcombing.

"I don't think I can." Laura mumbled something about having to be back home for tea, but the other boy with the lip piercing cut her off.

"That's what you get from living like a nun, all stuck up."

Annie swore at him. "Shut up. It's not her fault she has to go there. Anyway they get to go clubbing in London all the time which is more than anyone does round here."

Laura felt remote. She was grateful to Annie defending her, but the gulf between them all was only going to widen. She could only imagine their derision if they found out she was dating her teacher.

19. In London

Supposedly going to visit Susie and her English relatives, Laura took the hours-long train from Cornwall to London. There was an overnight sleeper train, exotically called the "Night Riviera" but Laura preferred to travel during the daytime. It was a chance to read, uninterrupted, for several hours. Or do homework: she had a tonne of Latin to translate over half term, Mr Tyrrell apparently not understanding the concept of a holiday.

This trip she found it hard to concentrate. She kept drifting into daydreams, even though she had treated herself by bringing a couple of her favourite books instead of school books.

She was nervous about seeing him again. Calabria had been so idyllic but as ever she worried that he would start getting over her, or not feel the same anymore.

* * *

Mr Rydell met her at Paddington railway station. She was overjoyed the moment she saw him, and she saw the same joy in his eyes. For a moment they just clasped one another and then he put his arm around her and they walked off to find a café and some food.

He was temporarily staying with a friend in North London, the same friend that had got him his current job. Although he owned a house in the South of England it was rented out because he was travelling so much, and it wasn't convenient to commute from.

"I would have booked us into a hotel, but Dean's going away for a few days to give us some privacy."

Laura was happier with this. It felt more normal, that they were staying together in a regular place and not sneaking around in hotels. More like when she had stayed with him in accommodation at Francis Hall. Hotels felt so temporary.

They took the underground to Dean's flat and Laura tried to remember the route. She had that wonderful feeling of the start of things, when all the time was stretching before them - all four nights of it, anyway - and every moment was something to be savoured.

Dean met them at the door and greeted Laura warmly. He was tall, around thirty, with straight, light brown hair. He also shot a look to his friend. "It's all starting to make sense now."

The second bedroom wasn't huge, this being London, but there was a double bed and you could see trees from the window. Albeit behind a lot of walls and the backs of other buildings, but at least there was some greenery and sky. Coming from Cornwall and all its wild expanse, Laura often felt a bit crowded in cities.

"What was that supposed to mean?" Laura asked, about Dean's remark.

"That you're incredibly beautiful and he can see why I've fallen for you."

It wasn't quite the whole answer, Laura felt. There was some other tone behind what was said, but she didn't push to find out now. She wondered if Dean had disapproved, due to the age gap or the circumstances. If so she doubted her appearance would entirely reassure him even if she was looking her best, which after several hours on the train she highly doubted.

Taking advantage of being along for a moment, Mr Rydell took her in his arms and kissed her. As ever her stomach flipped when his lips met hers and she arched up towards him, already wanting him.

He slid a hand over her jeans, between her legs, and she pushed against him.

"Do you want me?" he asked.

"Yes."

"I'm going to make you wait." There was a mocking glint in his eye. Laura understood that it might be rude to Dean if they locked themselves away immediately, but his superior self-control still irked her.

She moved her hand over him, feeling the rock hardness under his clothes. "Don't you want me too?"

"So much it's painful. But I'm still going to make you wait."

It was a threat as much as a promise. Laura shivered inwardly, wondering what he had in store, and let him lead her back out to the living room.

There, she sat down on the sofa, where Dean indicated, and was given a cup of tea. It was a nice flat. There was a real fireplace albeit with an electric heater in it, with bookshelves either side. You could tell that two men lived here, but not in a bad way. There weren't socks and things strewn about the place. They were obviously both quite organised.

"What plans have you two got for the weekend?" Dean asked.

Laura honestly didn't know. She wanted to visit more of the sights, maybe the Natural History Museum.

"There are some discount cinema vouchers if you want, by the phone. I don't know if anything decent's on though."

"Thanks. We'll probably stay in tonight, as Laura's spent over five hours on the train."

"I'm okay if you do want to go out," Laura said. "I'm not tired or anything."

"We might get some food then, instead of takeaway. Why don't you join us?" he asked Dean.

"I can't, I'm seeing Mel, but thanks for the offer." Mel was his girlfriend, she worked for an advertising agency. They had met in some bar and there was an anecdote about Dean taking Mel's drink by accident or vice versa.

Laura felt a bit overawed by the thought of it all. Here was Dean, going out with some doubtless sophisticated and professional woman probably near his own age, and here was she, just a schoolgirl. All these people were independent, grown up, they lived in London, worked and travelled all over the place. Her spheres of experience were Francis Hall and Cornwall.

She liked Dean, but she felt relieved when he finally went out and it was just the two of them. She went over the sofa and wrapped herself around her former German teacher. She felt that she would feel on a level with him again if they could make love.

This time she initiated the kiss, loving the fact that she had uninterrupted access to him. She pushed her hands through his hair and kissed him down the side of his neck. She tasted the warmth of his skin, smelt that intoxicating maleness that nothing could simulate except being with him.

"I was determined to wait until tonight but you don't make it easy, do you?" he said.

With his hand he cupped her breast over her top, brushing his thumb across. Laura caught her breath, Even his touch through fabric set her nerves tingling.

She wanted him badly. She wanted it hard. She wanted him to throw her down on the floor, and use the firmness of it to do her as hard as he could.

"I can't wait until tonight," she told him.

"Tell me what you want, then."

Laura never found this easy, but the reaction she got from him when she expressed what she wanted made the effort worthwhile.

"I want you to take me here, on the floor. Really hard." She was nervous saying it, but any doubt she felt was washed away by the dark heat she saw in his eyes.

"How hard?"

"As hard as you can."

"Hard like I need to punish you for something?" he asked. "Have you been up to anything?" He was peeling off her clothes as he spoke.

"No, I just need it. I need you." She needed him to absolutely make her his, to confirm that everything was okay. Plus physically it had been weeks since they had been together. She felt pent up.

Now he pulled her jeans down and off her, roughly. "You want me to fuck you hard? Are you sure you can take that?"

She felt a momentary flicker of something she couldn't pin down. It wasn't quite fear. But the look in her eyes gave him his answer. He had wanted her submission and now he had it.

He ran his hand between her legs, slipping just inside to felt how wet she was for him. For a moment he toyed with her, his finger tracing around her nub lightly, just not giving her quite enough pressure but making her throb with frustration.

He was still making her wait. His mouth went over her breasts, his tongue teasing her nipples, kissing her down her stomach. Stopping just before he went too low. He could tell that one flick in the right place would bring her over, and he didn't want it to happen too quickly.

Laura was dizzy with desire. He made her open her thighs for him, wide, his hands gripping her flesh, and she felt no shame. She was his. He was in command of her again.

Then he drove into her, as hard as he had ever done, her hips pushed hard onto the floor. He entered her so deeply it hurt as his full length bottomed out in her. She gasped, but she knew she had asked for this and he didn't plan to show her any mercy.

He also angled his body up so she couldn't press against him: he wanted her to come from the penetration alone.

It was wordless. It was a battle. They both wanted to prove a point.

Laura wanted to show that she could take anything he could give her, that she could never get enough of him.

And he wanted to remind her, as ever, that she was his. That he loved her above all others and she belonged to him alone.

She felt the force of him pushing her into the floor. Felt her skin drag on the carpet. She would have marks there afterwards.

"You want me to go even harder?"

She didn't think he could do, but he did. Deeper as well. It was making her cry out as well, in a strange fusion of pleasure and pain. He was stretching her, making her fit him.

"I'm not stopping until you come. You asked for this."

He was so much taller than her, so much stronger. Just the thought of how he was pinning her down bought her to the edge.

He was in control, so she could lose it. And she did. As her whole body spasmed around him he just kept driving and driving into her. His very hardness prolonged her sensations.

Afterwards she was tender, bruised, spent. He was exhausted. He collapsed on top of her, weighing her down against the floor and they both lay there, together but strangely apart.

20. Loved up

He was infinitely tender to her that night. When they finally got up and showered, and went out for food he treated Laura almost as though she were fragile.

As much as the rough sex had created a kind of awkwardness it had brought them closer together. It was the mutuality: that they both shared this desperate, crushing need.

He had suggested getting a takeaway but Laura preferred to go out. She loved being with him in public and the way it made it feel official.

They went to a restaurant and then to a bar. Laura wore her Italian dress and had a lot of men eyeing her up. She only really knew of it because Mr Rydell would get tense.

One time he was getting them more drinks when some guy tried to chat her up at the bar, which was very awkward. "Thanks, but I'm here with someone" didn't seem to cut it as the other guy was very drunk.

"Come on, have some fun!" he said, slurring his words. He even put his hand on her thigh which nearly caused a fight. She had to physically drag Mr Rydell away to stop him decking the guy.

"He was just some drunk idiot," she said afterwards.

"You attract a lot of attention and sometimes it's not easy. I don't mean it's your fault, but I can't be there most of the time. I worry about you," he told her.

"I'm imprisoned at Francis Hall most of the time so you really have nothing to fear. The only male who ever crosses the threshold of Michaelmas House is Jenkins." The school handyman was in his sixties with a wife and multiple grandchildren, and not an object of anyone's romantic intentions.

Mr Rydell wasn't entirely appeased, but it helped.

But the truth was that he also got attention. Perhaps less so in bars - there always seemed to be more predatory males than females - but out in the street Laura had seen women eyeing him up. He seemed completely unaware of the fact. She didn't want to keep pointing it out in case she sounded jealous.

In fact it gave her a thrill, to think that she was so lucky to be the one he had chosen, though it also reminded her how much competition was out there. His obliviousness to it assuaged her fears a little.

Dean was still out when they got home around midnight. He had said he would be back at some point, instead of staying over with his girlfriend, as he had to go to the airport fairly early in the morning.

Laura didn't mind as they would have several more nights together just the two of them, and she liked the fact that she had finally met one of his friends.

When they got back Mr Rydell shut and relocked the door. "Dean won't be back before two in the morning, he never is."

He turned to her. "Now take your clothes off. All of them."

Laura laughed initially. "Here?" They were in the living room.

"Yes. He won't be back for ages."

Wondering what he had in mind she took off her shoes and dress and stood there in the Italian lingerie. She heard him draw in his breath.

"That too. All of it. I want you completely naked," he instructed.

Strangely Laura felt self-conscious taking off the underwear as well. She wondered if he intended that, if he wanted to put her at unease for some reason. The thought of what he might do to her was already making her shiver with anticipation.

"Now close your eyes and keep them closed."

She obeyed. Doing so made her more aware of her body and her nakedness, but also vulnerable. He had made her stand once before but not quite like this. Not with her eyes closed. She could have cheated and kept them open but she was curious what he wanted. She also wanted to please him.

"Clasp your hands behind your back."

Laura did so. Her normal instant, naked, with her eyes shut, would have been to cover the front of her body with her arms. But he wanted her fully uncovered. Fully exposed to him.

She waited for what seemed like ages. Was he looking at her? Studying her? She could almost imagine

Then she felt his breath on the back of her neck, then his lips kissing her down her spine. Warm each time he embraced her skin, slowly, then a coolness in each abandoned spot as he moved lower.

She cried out as he reached the curve of her waist, trembling, her skin tingling with strange delight.

Then he must have drawn away, because she felt nothing.

She could hear him move in front of her. She longed to open her eyes but held them fast shut. Not knowing where he might touch or kiss her made all of her skin feel extra sensitive.

She could feel the heat of his body when he was nearer to her, although he wasn't touching her. Suddenly his mouth was over her breast, his tongue swirling around her nipple, making her moan. She could feel it tighten into a taut bud in his mouth. Her nerves were electrified by his teasing.

He broke off again and she felt the coldness of air where he had left her skin wet.

He did he same to the other side. Sucking on her gently, teasing her with his tongue, even biting her, but very gently.

Laura longed for him to caress her with his hands, cup her breasts. She wanted his warm, firm fingers on her body.

She was ridiculously hot and throbbing between her legs. Desperate for him to kiss or touch her there.

Instead she sensed him rise and stand in front of her. Finally his hands were on either side of her head, tilting it up towards his. "Keep your eyes closed."

His lips came down on hers and she opened for him, allowing his tongue inside to probe her, drink her. So warm, wet and intimate. She still yearned for the full, hard heat of his body against hers.

Then his head was at her knees and his was kissing up her thigh. He gripped her legs just above the knees, forcing them apart so he could kiss the interior of her thigh.

Closer, closer. She wanted him higher, right where she needed it.

But instead just as he reached the top of her inner thighs, when she felt sure he must start to give her the close contact and release she craved, he was kissing her lower belly and up the centre, between her breasts.

Laura groaned in disappointment. He said nothing, but she sensed he was pleased with her reactions to his touch.

His lips moved round her neck, drawing in the skin. If he gave her a love bite she would have to hide it back at school.

Then, telling her not to open her eyes, he picked her up and carried her into the bedroom. She realised where she was when he laid her on the bed and turned her over on her stomach. He pulled so her legs were on the floor and she was bent over the bed.

Finally his hands moved firmly to her upper thighs. He forced them apart and she felt his hardness press against her opening. She was so wet now, her flesh so swollen and aching for him that she couldn't have resisted anything, even though she was still sore from earlier.

He pushed into her, slowly, smoothly. All the way.

Deeper than it usually felt. Almost uncomfortably deep. She could feel herself stretched around him, and as he pressed to the hilt he held her there, rocking into her without withdrawing.

"You were made for me," he whispered. "You were made to fit me, exactly. Perfectly. Like this."

At that moment Laura thought she might die if he ever withdrew from her. It was like a key in a lock: she had a space inside her, and Mr Rydell filled it.

With him inside her like this, pushed into her to the utmost possible, she felt owned. She belonged to him.

Now he was grinding his hips against her in a slow circle, moving himself inside her but still not withdrawing.

Deep, deep, deep. They were connected. He pushed against her and inside her repeatedly.

"You belong to me, Laura. You belong with me."

Afterwards she never knew how long he made love to her like that. The strange, insistent pressure. It may have been minutes or an hour. Barely moving in and out of her at all.

128

She could feel him grow harder and thicker within her. Then finally he was coming, thrusting longer lengths inside her, increasing the pressure. On and on and on.

When he finally eased, he didn't rest as she had expected. Instead he flipped her over and his mouth went between her legs. He knew she hadn't reached release and he did not want to deny her.

It took few seconds of his mouth covering her, hot and warm, his tongue lapping firmly up against her nub for Laura to start bucking and clutching his hair as she came. He had wound her up for so long, she was as taut as a drum.

When he suddenly sucked on her most sensitive spot with more pressure than he had ever used before, it was the most exquisite agony she had ever known. She was overstimulated: a lost, spasming bundle of nerves, she thought she wanted him to stop but he didn't.

Yet she just as she was coming down from the first orgasm and his attentions were almost uncomfortable she found herself climaxing a second time. It was a different feeling, more focused between her legs, more intense, more draining.

They had never managed this before, and Laura had never felt so dizzy afterwards. Unable to speak, unable to move, she lay there with her eyes closed and let the blackness wash over her.

21. Domestic bliss

Laura woke to the smell of eggs and bacon frying, another lovely reminder that she wasn't at school. She was completely happy. Lying in the arms of the man she loved most in the world, safe from the outside world, school, her parents: all the forces that might conspire to separate them.

Feeling bleary she showered before joining the two men in the kitchen. "How do you like your eggs?" Dean asked.

Laura didn't mind. Any way would be better than eggs at Francis Hall. After the energy she'd spent last night she needed sustenance.

The conversation turned to the previous evening. "You and Mel go anywhere interesting?" Mr Rydell asked.

"We were supposed to meet her sister at some club. The queue was hours long, then we couldn't get in without being on a list. Totally wasted night," Dean said.

"Which one?" Mr Rydell asked.

Dean named the club. "It's in Mayfair," he told Laura. "So no wonder it's exclusive. Mel's sister got on some kind of guest list."

It was the same club that Laura had gone to with Susie and Charlotte. She felt awkward for having got in when Dean hadn't.

"Yes, I know it," Laura said. After all it was pretty famous.

"You know it well?" Mr Rydell asked. He was joking, assuming she had no acquaintance with it except the name.

Now Laura felt doubly awkward. Given she had meant to tell him at some point, it was now or never. To conceal it would look odd. "We went there once."

Both men looked very surprised.

"You went there?"

"Susie dragged Charlotte and me there last exeat. I never thought we'd get in either as we had no ID, but they just waved us through. I expect it was a quieter night," Laura said to Dean, feeling bad that she'd got in so easily while he and his girlfriend had wasted their time queuing.

Mr Rydell laughed, still looking shocked. "That girl." He meant Susie.

"Girl?" Dean asked.

"One of Laura's friends. The one who invited us to Italy. Something of a wild child," Mr Rydell told him.

"So what was it like?" Dean asked.

"Dark, crowded. I think the drinks were very expensive but Susie paid. She has some credit card her uncle gave her," Laura explained.

"Anyone famous there?"

Laura named the popstar and the band they'd seen. "We actually got invited to a party with them afterwards, or Charlotte did."

"But you didn't go?" Dean asked.

"Yes - no - we did go. It wasn't that great though." Laura was trying to play it down because she could see from the expression in Mr Rydell's eyes that he wasn't entirely happy with it all. She was anxious what he might say to her after Dean had gone.

Dean piled his plate into the sink. "Mel's sister would be green with envy. She's one of their biggest fans," he said, referring to the band. "Anyway, plane to catch, so I'd better get moving."

He went out to his room and Mr Rydell and Laura were left in the kitchen, a tense silence between them.

"Charlotte also had some woman approach her about doing modelling," Laura said, to try and shift the subject away from the party. "Earlier that day, when we were in Oxford St. She had a test photoshoot earlier this week."

It didn't work. The minute Dean left through the front door Mr Rydell went straight to the issue of their night out.

"Exactly what have you been up to?"

Laura didn't think she had done anything wrong, but somehow she also felt guilty.

"Really nothing. We just went to this party in some big house. I was with Susie most of the time. We crashed there and got the train back to Francis Hall the next morning."

"Most of the time?"

Laura tossed a mental coin. Should she or should she not tell him about Susie and the popstar? She wasn't sure if Susie's outrageous behaviour would make her own seem better or worse to him. She decided transparency was best, in case it all came up again later.

She gave him a basic overview. How Charlotte had been with the bass player for most of the night, but nothing had really happened except sitting around smoking a joint. How Susie had briefly kissed the popstar but he had been far too out of it for anything to happen. How she, Laura, had briefly talked to some London girl before joining Susie again and crashing in one of the bedrooms.

Mr Rydell didn't look pleased. "Anyone try it on with you?"

"Yes, but I wasn't interested, obviously."

He looked at her for a long moment. Laura felt as though she were on trial. And part of her felt resentful as she had done nothing wrong and it hadn't even been her idea or decision to go.

"I worry about you. Even when you're not doing things like this," he told her.

Laura's resentment melted. "I was fine, honestly. I was pretty much sober the whole time."

"Come here." He got her over to him. Pushed her hair back from her face as he held her. "You need to have fun. Enjoy your freedom. I never want to stand in the way of that. It's just kind of disconcerting to hear this stuff."

Laura looked into his eyes. The dark grey that showed concern. Possessiveness. A flicker of jealousy, a flicker of admiration. He was conflicted.

"I would rather have been with you," she told him.

"Would you?" There was amusement in his eyes too now, alongside the worry.

"More than anything." It was true, every precious day she had away from school that she didn't get to spend with him felt like a waste.

132

"Would you like to prove that?" There was heat in his gaze now.

Laura wasn't exactly sure what he wanted, but she sensed that he wanted her to submit to him in some way. She also wanted to prove to both of them that he was hers, and she was his. That no one else registered. Not the guys at the party, not even famous guys, not anyone.

She dropped to her knees and unzipped him. She was half surprised, half not-surprised that he was already rock hard. Loosening his fly she grasped him and took him into her mouth. He breathed in sharply. "Laura…"

She felt him twitch as she swirled her tongue around the tip of him. She wanted to take him deeper into her mouth but he was so large it was difficult. Freeing him more, and using both her hands, she cupped him and held him and tried to build up a rhythm.

She could tell it was working because he groaned as she reached a certain pace. His fingers, which had been gently twisting her hair, now pressed her head more firmly against him.

He was rocking into her, still small movements, but gradually setting the rhythm.

Now he had both hands either side of her head and he was moving her on and off him, going just a little deeper. Laura did what she could with her tongue, tried to add pressure with her mouth and draw him in. She wanted to win this. She wanted to make him lose control.

"Put your hands behind your back." It was a command, not a request.

Doing so, she had less control over the depth than when she had been able to hold him. But he didn't need that, he was holding her head and using her mouth as he needed. It was deeper than comfortable; she became anxious about how far he might go.

She knew he would never hurt her or push her too far, but the slight fear made her throb for him. His need for her, his use of her, aroused her. She felt a strange pride that she could do this for him.

He was thrusting into her faster, further and as the movement picked up pace he suddenly pushed much deeper and held her head onto him. It was probably only a few seconds but Laura felt panic and struggled. He was filling her, the hot firm length of him pushing past the back of her mouth.

At first he continued to hold her there. Then as soon as he realised it was too much for her he released her and she gasped in breath.

Then he pulled down her clothes and pushed her over the arm of the chair. She knew he was close and he desperately needed release so she let him position her, thrust into her.

Laura was already more than wet for him As always she wanted him, needed him to fill her. He knew she could take this and he didn't care about being gentle.

It was hot, raw need.

In less than a minute he was spasming into her, thrusting to the hardest and fullest, gripping her hips back against him.

When he was done he stayed inside her, still hard. Somehow he manoeuvred her around so she was now facing him, moving her leg up and between them both so he remained within her throughout.

Their eyes met. His were haunted, troubled, still desiring her.

Laura felt conflicted: both troubled and aroused. But she wanted him more than ever.

As if knowing what she needed, his gaze not leaving hers, he brought his hand between them. His fingers slipped down and he moved them slowly, slowly around and between.

She had craved his touch there so much that she actually whimpered when he brushed across her clitoris.

Still she kept her eyes on his, even as her breathing increased and the waves started to run through her.

The pressure was so direct he brought her to orgasm almost instantly. She felt her skin flush, her head feel light as the core of her tensed and spasmed. She wanted to close her eyes but she couldn't break the connection as he looked at her.

Laura had never felt more vulnerable or more exposed as she came. Or more protected. There was love in his eyes, and pride: both for his command over her as well as her ability to meet his desire, and yield to her own.

22. Attentions renewed

After a glorious couple of days Laura caught the train back to school. Mr Rydell wanted to drive her but she thought it would be too risky. People might actually recognise him: it wasn't as though she could claim he was her cousin or anything.

She hated leaving him again but at least it was only a few weeks until the next exeat which they obviously planned to spend together. The whirl of school swept her up as usual which helped take her mind off things.

Laura sat in the courtyard with Margery after lunch, enjoying a rare shaft of winter sunlight. Susie had been waylaid somewhere and Charlotte was doing something with her hockey boots.

Tom Hollier came past. "Sunbathing?" he asked, with a smile.

"It's the warmest we've been all term," Laura told him.

"They're not exactly generous with the heating here, are they? Makes me glad I didn't take them up on an offer of accommodation within the school. I can blast the heating when I get home at night," he said.

Laura had flashbacks to the previous term. The accommodation the school would have provided would probably have been the groundsman's cottages where Mr Rydell had stayed. She still got pangs when she walked past them remembering the time she had spent with him there.

She grimaced at Tom Hollier. "Don't rub it in. Our dorm is like something that monks would have suffered in the Middle Ages."

"You'll be well acclimatised for the Duke of Edinburgh award expedition then, won't you?" He had arranged for the practice expedition to take place towards the end of term. They were all dreading it.

"I can't see why we have to do two camping trips," Margery said. There were few things she abhorred more than camping.

"It's the rules, I'm afraid. Minimum one practice expedition. And more if you make a mess of it." He was clearly amused by Margery's antipathy, being an outdoors lover himself. Tom Hollier always looked incredibly rugged and healthy, Laura thought, no wonder he'd got so many Valentines.

Margery shuddered at the prospect of further nights under canvas. She was hoping there was some way she could avoid the expedition altogether. "It will get in the way of mocks," she said, referring to their practice exams.

"It will do you all good to get a break from your books. Besides, you can always take study notes on the coach. And in your backpack if you want. Take extra batteries and you can study by torchlight all night."

He was teasing Margery now but it wasn't far from the truth of what she would probably end up doing.

"Anyway, in addition to your Duke of Edinburgh practice trip there's an inter schools orienteering competition in a couple of weeks. On the Saturday," Tom Hollier said.

This would be the last exeat of term. As much as Laura was now finding some enjoyment in orienteering, there was no way she was going to give up a chance to see Mr Rydell and instead go tramping round muddy fields and woodland against hearty competitors from rival schools.

"We have a family event over exeat," she said. "I really can't miss it." She felt her face grow warm at the lie.

He looked disappointed. Laura wondered if he could tell she wasn't telling the truth.

"That's a shame. I thought we stood a good chance to come in among the top few, maybe even win, if you were leading the Francis Hall team," he said.

Laura felt even more guilty but Mr Rydell simply eclipsed everything.

"Maybe next time?" she said. "If there are other competitions?"

"There will be. I'll hold you to that," he said and went on his way.

Margery waited until he was out of earshot. "He'd better not figure out that you live in Cornwall and never go home for exeat," she said.

"I might go home though, if there was a family event."

"I suppose you might. But you'd better hope he doesn't mention it to Gi-Gi or something and she starts asking you questions," Margery said.

Laura thought this was unlikely. Partly because she was fairly sure he'd read the lie in her eyes. To mention it to her housemistress would expose her and she didn't think he was that sort of person. After all he hadn't breathed a word about their illicit pub expedition on the first orienteering outing.

* * *

"There was a phone call for you," Teresa Hubert announced to Charlotte when she saw her at Michaelmas House later that evening.

"Oh?" Charlotte tried to hide her alarm. She was worried it was the modelling agency. She was already stressed because they'd been given absolutely nightmarish maths homework. As a result she was trying to find Mary Rudge, who was good at maths, to give her some pointers.

"A very odd sounding man. Certainly not your father or that rugby captain from St Duncan's. He sounded more like something from the East End." Teresa was simultaneously digging and sneering. "I took the call, you see. The phone rang just after I finished speaking with my parents, some chirpy Cockney asking for you."

What Teresa described as "Cockney" could only be Tony the bass player, though he was actually from Essex, north east of London. So many weeks had elapsed since the night of the party that Charlotte had no longer expected to hear from him, and had found herself more relieved than disappointed.

Though of course it was always nice if a guy called, since you wanted him to be interested in you even if you didn't reciprocate.

So Teresa's news brought Charlotte mixed feelings. She also wanted to nip Teresa's nosiness in the bud. "It was probably my cousin," she said.

"Really?" Teresa arched her thin black eyebrows. There was an assumption that most people's relatives wouldn't have regional accents, unless they were foreign like Susie's mother or Scottish or something.

"They're from Essex." Charlotte looked at Teresa defiantly, daring her to make a snobby remark about the imaginary cousins.

"I'm sure it's a very nice place," Teresa said. Her tone suggested the exact opposite.

Charlotte was getting irritated. "So? Did you take a message?"

Teresa smiled, pleased that she had rattled one of her enemies. "You don't have your own cousin's number? Luckily for you that I wrote it down then. It's in the usual place." This was a notepad pinned to the wall by the payphone.

"Thank you." Charlotte spoke through gritted teeth.

"He didn't mention he was your cousin," Teresa said, trying to make one last stab.

"I don't imagine he had time to go through the entire family tree," Charlotte said. She turned and increased her pace so she could catch up with Susie and Margery. Laura was off in the clouds somewhere.

Charlotte could feel Teresa's unpleasant smile on her back as she walked off. Their nemesis had scored one tiny victory, however small.

And she would keep sniffing and digging until she had even more ammunition. They would have to be careful: there was a lot at stake.

* * *

English brought new trouble. Mr Peters, having spent the last half term focusing his attentions elsewhere, returned from the break with his ardour once more aflame for Susie. She had hoped his reeking Valentine might be the end of it.

He was once again all oily and obsequious charm. They were reading Under Milk Wood and Mr Peters cast Susie as Mae Rose

Cottage who *"draws circles of lipstick round her nipples"*. As the narrator, Mr Peters read this section with ill-concealed relish.

Perfectly composed, Susie read her lines with a fair attempt at a Welsh accent. *"I'm fast. I'm a bad lot. God will strike me dead. I'm seventeen. I'll go to hell."*

Teresa Hubert sniggered and muttered something to one of her neighbours, triggering a venomous glare from the English teacher.

The result was that Charlotte, who had to recite the Reverend Eli Jenkins' poem shortly afterward, couldn't keep a straight face. Laura was practically having to hold her breath to stop laughing.

Charlotte totally lost it at the phrase *"touch-and-go"* at which point Mr Peters lost his patience and ordered both her and Laura out of the room.

"This immaturity when reading a great work of literature is unacceptable," he told them, his voice tight with fury. He had some awareness that they may have been laughing at him which intensified his ire.

Outside Laura and Charlotte were doubled over nearly crying with laughter, before sobering up as they appreciated the trouble they might be in.

"Will he tell Mrs Grayson?" Laura asked.

"I hope not," Charlotte said. "But if another teacher comes by and finds us here, we'll get another grilling. Where can we hide?"

There was a nearby storeroom so they slipped in there to wait out the hour.

Laura wondered what Susie would do to get out of it. Of course she would hardly find herself in this position to start with, she was so slippery. "We'll just apologise profusely," Laura suggested. "Hopefully he'll let it go." Neither of them wanted any house demerit points which could be doled out for such an offence.

As it was Susie managed to butter up Mr Peters for them. "I'm so sorry, Sir, it was my accent. I was practising it last night to prepare, and Charlotte's grandmother is Welsh so it sounded funny to her."

Mr Peters, relieved not to be the butt of the joke and flattered by the thought of Susie doing extra preparation for his class, was mollified. "Your accent sounds quite fine to me, Susannah. Most melodious."

This time Susie had to bite her lip hard not to laugh.

Combined with Laura's and Charlotte's sincere-sounding apologies when they returned to clear their desks when the bell rang, Susie's efforts were enough to avoid further penalty.

The downside was that Mr Peters interpreted Susie's attitude as giving him the green light to renew his attentions. He was going to be a problem yet again.

23. A scare

Susie, perceptive as she was, could see that Laura was anxious about something. She was more distracted than usual, despite having come back from half term completely loved up over Mr Rydell. And presumably looking forward to seeing him the following weekend. There was another exeat and Laura was again planning to pretend to stay with Margery but actually slip away to London.

"Do you want a tea?" Charlotte asked Laura for the third time, as Laura seemed to be zoning out.

"What? Yes, sure, thanks."

Charlotte frowned but slipped off her bed and went downstairs to make some for herself and the others.

Susie eyed Laura thoughtfully.

"Something's up, isn't it? What wrong?"

"It's nothing. I'm fine," Laura said. But Susie could see from Laura's quick glance at Margery that there was something the matter, just not something she wanted to reveal to Margery. Which probably meant a problem with Mr Rydell.

Fortunately Margery soon went out of the room herself as she needed to get a book from someone. Once she had gone, Susie turned her attentions to Laura.

"So what is it? Don't pretend it's nothing, it's obvious that something's worrying you. Has your man gone AWOL?" she asked.

"No." But he might, Laura thought, if her fears were realised.

"It's not your family, is it?"

Laura put her head in her hands and for one awful moment Susie thought that something had happened to them. But then

Laura looked up again. "I'm late." She looked at Susie, assuming she would understand.

Momentarily Susie thought that Laura meant she was late with homework or an essay, because everyone was constantly late with everything these days. They all had far too much work on. "Late for...?"

"I'm never late. It's been four days." Four days when this entire, agonising future had been stretching before her of shame and condemnation and his anger and her parents' grief. Her imagination had been running wild.

"Oh God, that." Now Susie instantly understood. "But four days isn't much, really. Have you taken a test?"

No. How could she? There hadn't been a chance to get hold of one. There was a vague rumour that Matron kept one or two in the cupboard for occasions when a sixth form girl came to her in worried tears. But Laura hadn't dared to ask anyone about it. Let alone actually approach Matron.

Susie tried to bolster her spirits. "If you're panicking, they say that often delays it." Susie was fairly sure this was an Old Wives' Tale but she thought there was no point Laura going insane with stress right now. "You're seeing him next weekend, right?"

Laura nodded.

"Then you get hold of a test then. You don't even need to tell him if you don't want to. Just say you need to get some tampons, or just say that you need to go to Boots and be a bit coy about it, and he'll probably assume it's for tampons. You can do them in the loo in a few minutes, the pregnancy tests I mean. He need never know," Susie said.

It wasn't the kind of thing Laura could keep from him though. She felt he would guess as soon as he saw her.

"Either way, he's a grown man, I'm sure he'll do the right thing. And if it does happen" - Susie stopped herself from saying if the worst happened - "then it's very early and you'll have lots of options. Not like my nonna's friend who didn't realise she was expecting until she went into labour. Of course they didn't have pregnancy tests half a century ago and girls didn't have the first clue how babies were made, in Italy anyway. But it's all very easy now. You don't even have to let your parents know, everything's kept very confidential."

Susie's stream of chatter was reassuring to Laura. Just having been able to share her terrible burden of fear and not-knowing with someone else had lifted the load.

Laura was still terrified about telling Mr Rydell, and she couldn't think how it might have happened as she had been taking her pill diligently. She never missed a day. She couldn't help feeling that if she was pregnant, it was some kind of divine punishment on her for being in this illicit relationship with him.

* * *

Something more exciting helped Laura forget her fears, or at least took the edge of them for a while. Charlotte received a large envelope in the post, branded with the eye-catching orange, blue and grey logo of the agency. It contained a draft modelling contract, an appointment invitation to visit the agency again for full portfolio shots, and a couple of prints from her initial photoshoot.

"They look brilliant!" Susie said. "You really have the look, don't you?"

The others crowded round to see. It was amazing how much a professional photographer, camera and lighting had managed to transform Charlotte. She was naturally pretty, but the photos cast her in an entirely new light. There were cheekbones, angles, bee-stung lips.

Susie turned the photo around. On the back was scrawled "Beautiful, cherie - Yves". "Who's Yves?" she asked.

"The photographer," Charlotte said.

"Do they always write that?" Laura asked.

Charlotte wasn't sure. "Probably. Just to be nice, I expect."

"What did he look like?" Susie wanted to know.

"Gorgeous." Charlotte looked at Margery who confirmed this.

"He was very French looking." This was high praise coming from Margery, who had a thing for the French as it was her strongest subject at school.

The others started to tease Charlotte but she shrugged it off. "The guy is literally surrounded by supermodels in underwear every day. You saw the pictures on the walls, Margery. Some of them were actually famous."

For a while they were all caught up with the excitement of it all, speculating wildly about Charlotte's future on the catwalks of Paris and Milan. It still seemed like a wonderful fantasy.

But Charlotte's face fell. "I can't do it though, can I?" she said. "This contract, it has to be signed by my parents. There's no way my father would agree, he'd freak out if he knew any of this."

Everyone fell silent. Susie picked up the contract and leafed through it. Laura saw her eyes gleaming in the way they always did when she was plotting.

"You know, it doesn't actually say your parents," Susie said. "It says 'parent or legal guardian'."

"How does that help?" Laura asked.

"Legally, while you're at Francis Hall, I believe Grace Grant is your guardian," Susie said.

This didn't seem to be much use. They were hardly going to persuade Grace Grant to take a trip up to London and conceal it from Charlotte's parents.

"What I'm thinking," Susie continued, "is that for now, all you really need is someone to sign in the name of Grace Grant. If they check in the phone book, they'll see that a Mrs Grace Grant does live at the address you stated. It buys you time anyway. Once you've got your first job and there's money on the table, I'll bet anything it will be a different situation with your parents. I mean turning down the agency is one thing, turning down Chanel or Dior, that's quite another."

This assumed that Charlotte instantly managed to land some huge modelling contract with some famous brand. Laura privately thought that something smaller would probably come Charlotte's way first.

"So where do we come up with Fake Grace Grant?" Laura said. "I know we can just fake a signature and send the contract off, but what if Charlotte needs to produce her? She'll probably have to attend the photo shoot."

Once again Susie had been considering this. "It's a pity Zia Viola isn't around because she'd be perfect and she'd love to play along. But what about your bass player, Charlotte? He's rung, hasn't he?"

Tony the bass-player had called and left a phone message for Charlotte again. Fortunately the Upper Sixth girl who had taken the call had no idea who he was or the band he played for, or it would have created a sensation and Charlotte would have faced some very sticky questions. She still hadn't rung him back.

"He must know someone who could stand in for Gi-Gi," Susie said. "I'm sure he wouldn't care less about the subterfuge."

It was an idea but still hugely risky. Charlotte also wasn't sure if she wanted to see the musician again. She was feeling keener on Julian these days and things might get complicated.

What she did know, and she was almost surprised at herself for the strength of her desire, was that she wanted to pursue the modelling opportunity. She had never considered being a model and even now didn't aspire to some glamorous life. Having visited the agency and got a sense of the huge scale of girls trying to make it, she fully imagined it would be nearly all hard graft and broken dreams.

But if she made it - if she actually got some work and earned some money - she could start getting more control over her own life. Right now the strictures of Francis Hall were a weird kind of freedom for her. She got to play hockey, her number one love, because it was compulsory.

If she lived at home her father would have likely forced her to take music lessons instead, and extra maths tutoring. He didn't hold women's sport in any regard. If he knew that Charlotte was secretly hoping for a career in sport he would go ballistic.

He must never, ever find out.

PART III

Parting

We, that did nothing study but the way
To love each other, with which thoughts the day
Rose with delight to us and with them set,
Must learn the hateful art, how to forget.

A Renunciation, Henry King

24. Second exeat

Laura was sick with worry when she caught the train to London that Saturday. Her period still hadn't come and she could barely eat or sleep. She wasn't sure whether her lack of appetite was due to stress or whether - more horrifyingly - it was a pregnancy symptom.

Susie had been as kind and supportive as possible. They hadn't told Charlotte or Margery about Laura's fears since Charlotte had enough of her own issues to deal with and Margery would have been even more stressed about it than Laura.

"If the worst happens," Susie said, "and you need to go somewhere completely discreet then don't for a moment worry about money or anything. We'll fix everything. And there's no point worrying until you've taken a test. You've eaten so little recently that it's hardly a surprise if you've skipped a month."

Laura thanked her. "I don't know what I'd do without you. I was going mad, bottling it all up by myself."

"Just remember it could be worse," Susie said. "Imagine if your father was Charlotte's dad."

On the train, half-empty due to being a Saturday morning, Laura somehow felt that she was being carried away from her previous life forever. She imagined a future of being a teenage mother - possibly a single mother - and by contrast there was Charlotte with an international modelling career, Susie jetting about the world being glamorous and Margery no doubt doing something successful as well.

There was no way she could keep it. If there was an it. She felt changed forever either way, but she didn't want to be pushing a pram at her age. She wanted to finish school, to go to university. Travel. Choose her own future.

And she wanted to be with Mr Rydell. Desperately. Forever.

Her fears of his reaction were even greater than her fears of seeing a positive line on a pregnancy test.

An elderly lady in a hand knitted woollen hat offered her a mint. "You don't look well, dearie. Are you feeling all right?"

Laura took the mint because her mouth tasted bitter from nerves. "I'm just a bit tired," she said.

"You make sure you wrap up warmly in this weather, or you'll catch a chill. Young girls these days, they don't seem to realise it's winter, some of the things they wear." The kind old woman clucked on and Laura let her thoughts drift on to how she was going to broach the subject. Maybe it would be better to pretend she needed some sanitary products and just deal with the worst if and when it eventuated?

She cursed the fact that she hadn't been able to get to a chemist. She even regretted not taking up Susie's daring suggestion to raid Matron's cupboard and see if there really was a test there. But getting caught in such an act... Laura physically shuddered.

Finally the train pulled into the station, its terminus. Laura grabbed her bag, fastened her coat and stepped out into the cold air. She always offered to catch a tube to nearer where Mr Rydell was staying but he always insisted on meeting her at the station.

There he was. Wrapping her into his arms, warming her inside his long winter overcoat.

"It may have only been a couple of weeks but I've missed you so much," he told her.

She smiled and closed her eyes as he kissed her, losing herself in him. But when she opened them again she found him looking down at her, concerned.

"Have you been ill?" he asked.

"No, why?"

"Because you're paler than ever and you look like they're starving you at Francis Hall."

Laura tried to laugh it off. "You can hardly expect a glowing tan in winter. And the food is awful, as you know."

He didn't look convinced. "While you're with me you're going to eat properly."

She loved that he cared about her. Even if his concerns were misplaced, as she usually had a healthy appetite, it was nice that he was looking out for her. She smiled and his brought his lips down on hers again.

"Let's go and get a hot drink and some lunch. You're half freezing," he said. He put his arm around her as they walked, and she loved the heaviness of it in his thick coat. Even though green shoots of spring were starting to appear the wind was bitter.

Inside a nearby café Laura ordered hot chocolate while Mr Rydell had coffee, and they both ordered toasted sandwiches. He insisted on paying. "While you're with me, I'm looking after you."

She would have liked to reciprocate but there was no opportunity for him to be "with her", so to speak. She didn't have a place of her own and as for him coming to stay at her parents' house, it couldn't even be considered. One day, though, things would be different.

The hot drink warmed her but she still had a sinking feeling in the pit of her stomach. She knew she had to broach the issue, she just wasn't sure how. For now she played for time, bringing up the story of Charlotte and her modelling adventures.

As always Mr Rydell found her friends' antics entertaining.

"So Charlotte plans to show up with a perfect stranger to fraudulently sign a modelling contract in the name of your housemistress?"

That was pretty much the situation. If it was needed, of course. Charlotte had rung the agency and fixed a date for the first week of the holidays which bought her more time. "The musician bloke she met thought it was a great idea. Of course he knows tonnes of models anyway so it didn't really phase him. He's getting his aunt to do it."

Tony had described his aunt as a "wicked old bird" who would be only too delighted to help.

"Have you considered what will happen when they post the finalised contract back to Grace Grant by return of post and she opens it?"

Laura had wondered about this. "We weren't sure if they would do that or not."

"I should imagine they will."

Poor Charlotte. There was every chance this might blow up in her face. She needed to land some amazing contract, quickly. "I guess we'll have to try to intercept the post," Laura said.

This wasn't necessarily as tricky as it sounded. It was a sixth former duty to supervise the distribution of the post in each house, roping in younger girls to actually sort it out and deliver it.

In reality they didn't pay much attention to what was going on and would likely be even more distracted by mock A-level exams when they got back.

Margery could volunteer to help, Laura thought. No one would ever suspect her. Then all she had to do was keep an eye out for anything addressed to Grace Grant - fortunately the agency used customised stationery - and surreptitiously put it into Charlotte's locker.

Laura explained this to Mr Rydell and he laughed.

"You've got it all figured out, haven't you? I suppose it's for a good cause. It's one of the top agencies after all, hardly some sleazy backstreet set up. Most people would be blown away by the prestige."

Not Charlotte's father though. Laura was glad Mr Rydell approved of the plan at least, or didn't seem to disapprove. She wasn't sure why his approval should matter to her but it did.

"Dean's away this weekend by the way, we've got the place to ourselves," he told her.

On the way back to the flat they passed a branch of Boots and Laura went in to get the test. When he asked her what she needed she had been so genuinely flustered that he had assumed it was female products, so Laura didn't even have to use the subterfuge that Susie suggested.

She was going to have to tell him anyway. Just not yet. It wasn't a conversation she wanted to have in the middle of the street.

Inside Laura had no idea where to look. She had thought that pregnancy tests might be near sanitary products but she wasn't quite sure what she was looking for: what the boxes looked like or even how big they were. It wasn't anything that she had had to find before, let alone buy.

She went up and down shelves, trying to find the right place. She felt completely out of her depth.

A nearby shop attendant asked her if she needed help, he was male which made her feel even more self-conscious.

"A pregnancy test," was all she managed to say.

He showed her to the correct shelf but there seemed to be several varieties and she had no idea which one to pick. "Do they all work the same?" she asked.

"Pretty much. This one is a two-pack, so you can test again in a few days. You can get false negatives from testing too early," the man said.

That was the last thing Laura needed to hear. Why oh why wouldn't her period just come? She vowed she would never resent its arrival ever again, no matter how much hassle it was or how bad the cramps were. It should be called the blessing, not the curse.

Feeling very out of her depth she shoved the supposedly discreet brown paper bag into her own bag. She was relieved she had taken some money from Susie who had warned her the tests could be expensive.

As they walked up to Dean's flat Laura was going over and over in her head how she would tell Mr Rydell. "I think there's something you ought to know..." "I've got something I need to tell you..."

Inside it was warm and he hung her coat up for her.

She stood there, clutching her bag, feeling panicked.

He saw the fear on her face. "What's wrong?"

"I'm late. I'm worried I'm pregnant."

25. The reaction

It was there, in his eyes, only for a split second before he suppressed it, replaced by concern, a frown, attentiveness, reassurance.

But Laura had seen it, and it was the last thing she had ever expected.

"I'm worried I'm pregnant."

She had anticipated that Mr Rydell's first reaction would be shock. Disbelief. Panic. Confusion. Something similar to how she felt. Even anger.

But not this.

Not the sudden flash of joy that momentarily, involuntarily lit up his eyes.

It was gone in an instant and she almost wondered if she had imagined it.

Except she hadn't. And they both knew it.

Laura knew that her own face would be stricken, scared, desperately hoping it was just an irregular cycle. Every fibre of her being not wanting it.

"How late is it?" he asked.

"Nearly two weeks." She wanted to cry, to burst into tears and to be in his arms, with him telling her that everything would be okay. But now there was this gulf between them.

Something that was horrifying to her was wonderful to him. Of all the things that divided them: age, status, life experience, nothing had ever felt so unbridgeable as this.

So she stood there, pale and tense, feeling almost as though they were strangers. He reached out to her but she didn't move to him.

"I've bought a test."

"Let's find out then, shall we? I love you, remember. Whatever happens, I'm here for you. Whatever you want to do I'll support you, you're not alone." She could see the concern in his eyes, the concern for her.

Only she was alone. Because what she wanted wasn't what he wanted, deep down. Realistically she knew he didn't actively want them to start a family right now. It would be absurd, it would wreck their lives. But if it happened by accident it wouldn't be as unwelcome for him as it would be for her.

Laura went into the bathroom. It was hard to open the packet because her hands were shaking from nerves. The packaging wouldn't seem to open, she couldn't manage to tear the plastic wrapping the indicator stick. It felt like it was resisting her but somehow she managed to extract it.

Then she had do what was required. She was so strung up that she couldn't even go for several moments.

When it was done she sat and waited. She knew he was outside, waiting too, but he didn't disturb her because he knew she needed her own space and time right now.

Laura read the test pamphlet to pass the time. As the man in Boots had said, it recommend taking a second follow-up test. But the main problem with false negatives appeared to be testing too early, and Laura was well past that stage.

She couldn't look at the test while she waited. She couldn't bear the idea of seeing a line appearing.

Finally the ten minutes were up.

White. Blank.

There was no line.

Laura stared at it as closely as she could, held it to the light, but there was nothing there.

No line. Not pregnant.

She felt like the heaviest burden ever had just been lifted from her shoulders. But instead of feeling drenched with relief, she felt numb.

For a while she sat in the bathroom, looking at the test just in case it changed, feeling that she had been given her life back. A second chance.

Eventually he knocked. "Are you okay?"

"It's blank."

He was silent for a moment. "Well that's a relief, if you're okay with it."

Laura was more than okay with it. The question was whether he was? Whether a tiny part of him was disappointed?

She couldn't look him in the eye when she first came out again. She showed him the test and he handed her a mug of tea.

"I'm sorry you had to go through this. We should probably start using extra protection," he told her.

He was really tender to her. They sat on the sofa watching television, Laura was lying against him with his arm around her. She felt safe, protected.

Bit by bit things started to feel normal again, or as normal as they could do given the circumstances.

"We're not the first couple to go through this," he said. "I realise how stressful it is, particularly the first time."

She thrilled inwardly at him using the term "couple". "Has this happened to you before?" They had never really talked about his past or his exes, but Laura had always assumed there must be a few. She wasn't worried about him still having feelings for them because she was confident in his affection for her, or confident enough. But she did worry from time to time how she compared.

"Not quite this close, but in my student days there were a few times we played it a bit close to the line. Drinking too much, not always using protection. A lot of bullets were dodged." He was smiling, trying to make light of it.

Except she knew he hadn't really seen it as a bullet in her case.

"If you're worried we can start using condoms as well. It's as much my responsibility as yours."

"Will it feel the same?"

"A bit different, but still amazing because it's with you," he told her.

Laura wasn't sure what she wanted. She wanted to forget this whole thing had ever happened. To fix this strange distance she felt from him.

"Given we only have this afternoon and tonight, and we don't need to spend it making doctor's appointments, what would you like to do?" he asked her.

They were in London so they had the entire city at their feet. There were endless touristy things that Laura would normally have loved to do. If the weather had been better she had thought about going on a boat trip on the river Thames to see Tower Bridge and Westminster from the water. It was something she hadn't done before.

But outside fell a cold, grey drizzle and she found herself thinking of a recent English lesson where they had covered pathetic fallacies. Mr Peters had droned on in his typically affected way while Susie rolled her eyes and pretended to strangle herself from boredom when he wasn't looking. Despite her gloom Laura smiled at the memory.

"Something amusing?"

"I was just thinking of Mr Peters."

Mr Rydell raised his eyebrows. "Really? A delightful reminiscence?" His tone was mock amused, he knew what they all thought of their English teacher.

"No, just Susie playing up behind his back." The thought of Susie somehow made everything seem lighter. Laura found herself half wishing she was with Susie now as she would cheer everything up within moments. But Susie was supposedly on one of her illicit sleepovers at St Duncan's, hiding out in Darius's dorm over exeat.

"Her luck will run out one day. It shouldn't be humanly possible to get away with what that girl does," he said when Laura mentioned Susie's exeat plans.

"I don't think her luck can run out. I mean even if she was caught, she wouldn't care. It would just be amusing for her. She'd enjoy it as another adventure."

The prospect of parental fury didn't faze Susie whatsoever. Charlotte was terrified of her father's reaction to any misdemeanour, and Laura would have hated to upset her own parents. She wished she didn't have to keep her relationship a secret from them. But Susie lived in a moral dimension all of her own.

"So what's it to be? A serious educational trip to a museum? Shopping? Do you want to go up Covent Garden and try and see a show? Failing that we could go to the cinema."

Laura decided that she would love this. Whether the theatre or a film, it would take her mind off things. "Covent Garden would be amazing."

"Great. A musical or a play? Or we can decide when we get there, depending what tickets are available."

Laura hugged him. "Either would be perfect." The future was starting to seem brighter. She wasn't pregnant. She had her future back. She was free and she was in the arms of the man with whom she was absolutely, completely in love.

* * *

They got dinner, saw a musical, went to a bar. When they finally staggered back to Dean's flat, Laura buoyed up by alcohol and her continued sense of relief, it was well past midnight.

"Everything's okay again, isn't it?" she asked him.

Mr Rydell silenced her by bringing his lips down on hers. Even as she felt her stomach flip at the warmth of his kiss she wished he had answered her verbally. She wasn't totally certain if this was his answer or if he was avoiding answering her.

Shortly afterwards he made love to her as though she was a fragile thing. He was slow and tender and infinitely gentle. He revered her with his body, telling her how beautiful she was, how much he loved her.

But even as he said these words Laura felt the new gulf between them. She worried that deep down, he was disappointed in her. Something in him had withdrawn from her and it was all her fault.

She had desperately wanted to sleep with him to blot it out, yet somehow his tenderness towards her only reminded her of their disparate reactions. She felt guilty that he was being so kind to her.

Laura wanted him to be less kind. She would have felt better if he was more dominant, she would have been more able to let herself go. She wanted him to take out the anger that she was sure he felt, to be rougher with her.

She bit his shoulder to taste his skin, tasted the salt of his sweat. She used her fingers to claw his back closer against her, trying to convey what she needed.

He was firm - he was always firm - he still commanded her body. He required her to climax with him and for him. As he moved inside her he slid his hand in between them, pressing his thumb over her sensitive nub.

She gasped as he pushed against her, manipulating her. She writhed against him, trying to lessen the pressure which was almost too much. She was over sensitive, over wired.

"Now, Laura."

He was gazing down at her, he loved to watch her face as she came. Tonight there was a new intensity in his eyes as though he had a point to prove.

"Now. Don't fight it." He was almost glaring at her, his hair damp against his forehead, his jaw set, willing her and ordering her to yield to him.

She knew he wouldn't stop until she let go. She wasn't even aware she had been fighting it, but as he spoke the words something inside her gave and everything felt like it was swelling, her skin flushing hot.

Her legs were dizzy and she was nothing but a pulsating centre of need, directly under his thumb, radiating out. Now she was reaching up to him even as she tried to twist away, trying to get just the right pressure. She was moaning, saying his name.

"Keep going." The flat of his thumb was even harder on her.

Laura felt everything rush and tip her over the edge. She came, the blood rushed to her head, the sound of her own rapid breathing drowned out. She closed her eyes to block out everything except how he made her feel. He was driving into her, prolonging her sensations.

Then her nerves became hypersensitive, she opened her eyes tried to pull away but he leaned on her more heavily. He still wouldn't remove his hand.

"And again."

He had never done this before, not let her rest, not let her recover. She didn't see how it was possible she could keep going. But as he continued to move inside her, rock hard and rigid, while his thumb rubbed and pressed - slow, firm strokes against flesh that could hardly bear any more sensation - she felt held against the edge.

"Christ, I just can't get enough of you." His pace was increasing: Laura wasn't sure if she could take much more.

Even as it was all too much she started losing control all over again. Shaking, shuddering, feeling him finally thrust hard and almost painfully deep within her as he climaxed. This time it was concentrated in the lower half of her body: sharper, followed by an even greater sense of exhaustion.

"Please hold me," she whispered as he withdrew from her. He pulled her against him, his chest against her back, his arms around her. She needed him. She loved him. She was still terrified she had ruined everything.

26. Relief and doubt

"I take it I don't need to start knitting booties?" Susie asked when Laura arrived back that evening. Susie was already in the dorm, Charlotte and Margery were elsewhere.

Laura smiled. "No. Thank God."

"I thought it was probably just a scare. Goodness though, imagine the scandal if it hadn't been!"

Now the worst was over they could joke about it but Laura still felt a hollowness inside. The world seemed tilted on its axis.

"Don't tell the others. I feel kind of stupid about it now," she said.

"Well, don't be. Scares happen, it's better that you took the test than left it too late. I mean if you were actually pregnant."

Laura put the contents of her weekend bag back into their various places. She felt like she was constantly packing and unpacking these days. "So how was your weekend? How was Darius?"

"We had fun." Susie's grin said it all.

Darius was so perfect for Susie, Laura thought, even if Susie never did seem to admit to any romantic feelings. He was very intelligent and laid-back with a cynical sense of humour, and just like Susie he couldn't care less about any kind of rules. His family was also rich, so he didn't have to worry about getting expelled anyway.

Susie was combing her hair. Laura envied the way her curls bounced back after being stretched straight, as soon as the comb left them. Susie had just the right amount of curl to her hair. Laura's own hair was dead straight so naturally she had always wanted the opposite. But perms were forbidden at Francis Hall along with dyed hair, make up and having more than one ear piercing.

"So, not long until the end of term. Just next weekend, then this awful Duke of Edinburgh camping trip with Tom and then we're free," Susie said.

"At least it's not as cold as it was." The early signs of spring gave some hope that the weather wouldn't be too bleak for their trip. "We were just talking about the Duke of Edinburgh camping trip," Juliet said to Charlotte and Margery, who had just entered.

Charlotte rolled her eyes. "Don't remind me. So long as you map-read we might survive."

"You're supposed to be the leader," Margery reminded her. She been working herself into something of a panic over the camping expedition.

"No one is going to know who reads the map or not. Besides, this is different to regular orienteering. We just have to find our way along a route and pitch our tents," Charlotte said.

Susie was filing one of her nails. "Darius and Julian have camped near where we're going to be. Apparently there are enormous slugs there, six inches long, nearly the size of bananas."

Margery shuddered. "Slugs don't get that big," she said.

"They do on the moors," Susie told her. "You wait and see."

Laura felt sorry for Margery. "We can put salt down around the tent. It kills them, the garden ones anyway."

"Or you can make a slug trap with a can of beer," Charlotte said.

"Just where are we going to get beer on the middle of the moors?"

"Tom might have some," Charlotte said. "Or maybe there's a pub somewhere."

But there wasn't. Laura had already been looking over the area maps to plan the route and there was nothing in the entire area. It was a literal wilderness judging by the map symbols.

"Oh well, never mind," Susie said. "I've got some vodka we can bring with us, if one of you can share your water flask with me I'll put it in mine."

"Where is it now?" Laura asked.

Susie held up a rubber hot water bottle and shook it at them so they could her the liquid swishing around. "Courtesy of Darius and Julian. They practically have a wine cellar under the floorboards of their dorm. Just don't let Matron empty this in the next two weeks."

Charlotte grimaced. "Won't it taste of rubber?"

"Probably. If we mix it with Coke it won't notice though."

* * *

The cold was finally lifting. Charlotte was still doing her early morning running but found it noticeably less freezing.

"How can you bear to get up in the dark?" Margery asked, not for the first time, when Charlotte joined them at breakfast one morning, having arrived late.

Charlotte shrugged. "It's awful but it's necessary, if you know what I mean."

Margery didn't. In her opinion nothing could be worth such an awful effort. It was hard enough getting out of bed on a cold morning as it was.

But Charlotte also had the modelling agency in mind. She was aware that most models had to keep thin, even underweight, and running was one way to stay as lean as possible while still being able to eat enough to have energy for hockey.

So far it was all good with signing the contract. Tony the bass player had been a big help there, bringing along some marvellous old Cockney aunt who had posed as Grace Grant and competently forged a signature.

"Do you think they'll post that contract back to you?" Laura asked. This was the big fear: that their housemistress would discover it first.

"Hopefully not. They gave us our copy then and there, but I don't if know there'll be some other letter posted," Charlotte said.

There hadn't been yet, but they were all trying to keep an eye on the post that arrived.

It was weird that Tony and Charlotte had become friends since he was quite a bit older than her, from a very different background, and they had nothing obvious in common. He seemed to enjoy the fact that they were all private school girls breaking the rules. Since learning Charlotte's actual age he hadn't even tried anything on either but had started acting more like a big brother.

"Maybe he's gay?" Susie said. "Not that I got that vibe, but you never know."

"I don't think so. He has a kid with some ex," Charlotte told her, spreading the last scrapings of a pot of marmalade on an already cold piece of toast.

"That doesn't mean anything. Look at Oscar Wilde," Laura pointed out. With Charlotte having finished the marmalade she reached for the honey jar. Unfortunately it was mixed through with old toast crumbs and did not look appealing. So she ate her toast plain instead, swallowing it down with tea. She hadn't heard from Mr Rydell in a few days which was normal - it was sometimes tricky making phone calls - but given everything that had happened she was feeling anxious.

"What's next then?" Margery asked Charlotte.

"They print the photos on this card, then they're going to start putting me forward for jobs which means I'll have to go to castings. God knows how I'm going to manage that with school. If it's in the Easter holidays it will be a lot easier." At least Charlotte didn't live as far from London as Laura did.

"You're always welcome to pretend to be staying at mine," Susie said. "It would be so much easier if Zia Viola kept a flat in London, but she prefers hotels. I may nag her to lease somewhere so I can escape there and annoy my parents. She'd like that. Then we could party there whenever we wanted."

"You'd never come back to school," Laura said.

"Quite possibly I wouldn't, no. Zia Viola wouldn't mind me living there."

Charlotte was dismissive. "They'd call Social Services on you. And what would you live off?"

"Poker, I expect," Susie said.

It was an absurd dream. Absurder still was the fact that they could all imagine Susie actually managing to do it.

* * *

Teresa had noticed the foursome having more furtive conversations as well as Charlotte in particular being alert for the post when it came. She was obviously expecting something and Teresa wondered what.

She decided to keep her own eyes open.

It was hard, since they were all as thick as thieves. It could just be something with one of their stupid boyfriends at St Duncan's but Teresa sensed that something more was going on. Susie in particular was so smug, Teresa hated her as much as she feared her.

What could it be?

Teresa took to looking in the pigeon holes to see if anything had been posted to any of the four of them. She might have missed the prize were it not for a stroke of luck in History one day.

Charlotte had been feeling increasing anticipation about the modelling agency posting something to Grace Grant. She was constantly checking the hall table outside the housemistress's study, where the post was kept, seeing if she could spot the modelling agency's logo.

By a stroke of fortune she was there after breakfast one day, right as the post arrived. She had forgotten a history book and had had to run back to Michaelmas House from the main school to pick it up.

The post van was just leaving as Charlotte came downstairs again with her book. The letters for that day were still in the wire box on the back of the door, jumbled up. Only sixth formers were allowed to remove them and sort them, but the box wasn't actually locked.

There, clear and bright on a large envelope was the agency's logo.

Quickly and silently Charlotte checked no one was around and fished out the incriminating envelope. Sure enough, it was addressed to Grace Grant. She stuffed it inside her textbook and ran back to the main school buildings, hoping she wouldn't be too late.

Mr Poynter, the History teacher, had a generally mellow disposition. Short and stout, he was earnest about his subject and well-liked. Charlotte apologised profusely for being late. "I'm so sorry Sir, I forgot my Modern World History."

Her teacher chuckled. "I hope you'll remember some of it in time for exams."

Charlotte took her place at the back. She was shaking with surprise nerves, the theft of the letter had rattled her. She also had no idea what she was going to do with it.

"What's wrong?" Laura whispered.

Charlotte opened the book a crack and showed her, at which Laura's eyes widened. Susie, on Laura's other side, could also see and grinned. "Thank God," she mouthed.

Teresa saw everything. From her angle she couldn't see what was in the book but she knew there was something there. It could of course be anything. Probably some shitty poetry that Charlotte had written to Julian. Or maybe a racy letter from him. The latter piqued Teresa's interest more than the former.

But it was Susie's reaction that really intrigued her.

They think they're so clever, she thought to herself. All their stupid secrets and sneaking around. This time Teresa was determined to discover what the game was.

27. Splitting up

"I can't do this any more."

The words hung in the air, they swirled and around, growing louder and louder.

The shock of it. The brute, blunt, shock.

"I can't do this any more."

But hadn't there been a tiny seed of doubt? A gnawing worm, a slight sense of apprehension that she had tried so hard to suppress.

Though it didn't mitigate the shock, it made it worse.

Laura sat slumped in the corridor by the payphone, near the door to Grace Grant's office. Her head was spinning.

In just a few seconds her entire world had fallen apart. She was numb, she couldn't take it in.

It was a Friday evening and she had managed to phone Mr Rydell. He had answered directly, often it was Dean who picked up the phone. The conversation had started the usual way on her side - "hello, how are you?" - she was so happy just to hear his voice.

He had sounded strange, stiff. "I'm good." Then a pause.

"Laura, I can't do this anymore."

What? The phone call? "Do what?" For a split second she had teetered on the edge of a precipice before he pushed her over.

"Us. It has to end. I can't go on like this."

"What do you mean?" Was he joking? Had something happened?

"I have... adored all the time I've spent with you." The fraction of a second pause, was he avoiding saying "loved"? "But it's not right. It never was, there are too many years between us."

She was starting to panic. He had never, ever said anything like this before. "It's not ever been a problem. I love you. It doesn't bother me."

"It bothers me. I should never have started it. It wasn't fair on you." His tone: so grave, so distant.

"But I love you. You're the only person in the whole world that I could feel like this about. I don't understand why you're saying this." Laura was pleading with him.

There was a pause and she heard him breathe in.

"Laura, I'm sorry, it's over."

What? "No! Don't be ridiculous, it can't be. I love you!" She was starting to feel sick. The world seemed to have nothing in it except for the heavy plastic phone receiver, the hard wooden parquet beneath her, her voice and his voice.

"You should be seeing boys your own age. Or just concentrating on your studies. This should never have happened, it's not right for either of us. We're at very different places in life."

He meant the pregnancy scare. He had been ready but she wasn't, and he had seen it. It was all her fault. If only it hadn't happened. If only she hadn't let him see her fear.

"I don't want to see boys my own age. I just want you. No one else could compare." Don't do this, don't do this. She was willing him to change his mind, to see reason.

She heard him breathe out, she heard frustration. "That's the problem. You have nothing to compare this to. How could you possibly know that you don't want anything, anyone else?"

"So what are you saying, that you want me to go out with different guys so I can decide if I like you best or not?" she asked.

"No - yes - you need to live your own life. I can't do this any more."

"Do you still love me?"

"You have an amazing life ahead of you. You'll see one day why this wasn't right."

"Do you still love me?"

He wouldn't answer her. "Laura, it has to be goodbye."

"Just tell me if you still love me." She was desperate, the entire world seemed to hang off the thread of him telling her he still loved her.

There was a pause again.

"Goodbye, Laura."

A click. Silence. He was gone.

She tried calling back but the phone was engaged. She tried again, several times. Had he left it off the hook?

As the realisation sank in the whole universe was crushing in around her, it was so heavy. She couldn't move. She could barely even breathe. If she could have stopped breathing, and let everything slip away, she would have.

* * *

Grace Grant, coming back to her office, found Laura sitting there, the phone dangling off the receiver from its cord. Laura was white, her arms wrapped around her legs. Her face half buried against her knees.

The girl had clearly received a terrible shock.

"Laura... is it your parents?"

Laura looked up at her housemistress. Wordlessly she shook her head but her eyes said it all. Grace Grant had seen this before, many times. Rarely of this intensity, though heartbreak in teenage girls was never easy. They took everything so hard, so very much to heart.

"Come into my office." Her tone was kind.

She ushered Laura in and sat her on one of the armchairs near the window. It was dark outside and Grace Grant drew the curtains. She busied about making some tea though she doubted Laura would drink it.

"I'm guessing that you've heard some bad news from someone you love?"

Laura nodded, miserably. She felt the weave of the armchair fabric beneath her fingers, the alternate rough and smooth where there was a pattern of silvery flowers.

"He ended it. I don't know what to do. I tried to call him back..." She trailed off, she was talking to herself as much as her housemistress.

Grace Grant patted her on the shoulder, knowing all too well how hopeless any comfort was at a time like this.

"I know it must seem like the end of the world. I should give you a lecture on busying yourself with your schoolwork and concentrating on your exams, but it wouldn't do any good, would it? I'm afraid this is something that just takes time."

"I love him."

"I know."

They both knew the name, but for both their sakes they wouldn't say it. They would keep up a pretence that it was some boy, pretend that the housemistress hadn't guessed that Laura had been seeing her former teacher.

"He wouldn't say if he loved me. He wouldn't tell me."

Grace Grant poured the tea from a large, brown pot. Everything seemed louder to Laura. The hollow way the liquid seemed to ring as it fell into the cup. The sound of footsteps and voices elsewhere in the house. The humming of something electrical, a lightbulb?

"I wish I could offer you some better comfort, dear." Her eyes flicked across to a photograph on her desk, of her own late husband. "All I can really say is that while there's life, there's hope."

Laura, who had followed the housemistress's gaze to the picture frame, looked back at her.

"Do you mean…"

"I don't mean that you should focus your whole life and happiness on getting a relationship back. What I mean is that while we are alive, there is always the chance of finding love again. Whether that's with someone new, or with someone from the past." The housemistress hesitated to say the latter, not wanting to give Laura false hope nor wanting to encourage a relationship that she felt was inappropriate.

But young women could be very melodramatic: everything was always all or nothing. Grace Grant had felt the same herself, many decades ago. She knew that right now all Laura wanted, the only thing that would keep her going, was the thought of getting her boyfriend back. In time that would change, and the girl would find meaning from other things.

For now, during this crisis, it was better to allow a pretence that the door was still ajar. One day, at least as Grace Grant fervently hoped, Laura would firmly close it herself and never wish to open it ever again.

Laura held the cup of tea in her hands, looking down at its surface. Her hands drank in the heat but she couldn't even sip it. She suddenly felt exhausted.

"Everything feels so heavy."

Grace Grant was all sympathy. "I know. You've had a very sad shock, I'm sure. If you want to go straight to bed I'll write you a note to excuse you any homework tonight."

Bed was exactly what Laura did want. She wanted to blot everything out. To wake up and find it was all just a terrible dream.

* * *

Laura fell asleep quickly but her dreams were tormented. They were filled with a sense of loss.

In her mind she was running through an endless field. She had lost something. Someone.

She was chasing them. But whenever she reached the place that they were, filled with a sense of relief and anticipation, they had already left and were far away. The panic and disappointment were like something crushing her.

"Where are you? Why do you keep leaving?"

When she finally woke in the early hours she felt bruised from the dream, though unknowing why. For a few numb seconds she didn't remember what had happened the day before.

The it all came crashing down on her. She curled into the foetal position, feeling the pain and emptiness overwhelm her. What was the point of ever getting out of bed again?

"Are you okay?" It was Charlotte, back from her morning run. They had all come in the previous night to find Laura already asleep. They had thought she might be ill and hadn't disturbed her.

Laura couldn't speak.

"Should I get Matron?" Charlotte was very concerned. She was even more shocked when Laura turned her face to her: pale and drawn with her eyes red from crying.

"No, I'm fine."

"You look terrible. Has something happened?"

Somehow it all came out. All her friends were there for her and somehow they held her together.

Margery, who had disapproved of the relationship, was surprisingly the most distressed. Bereaved herself, having lost her mother, she understood loss more than the others did. She remembered the sense of panic, of being abandoned. Of no going back. Of all of them she was the first to offer hope.

"He's still out there, and maybe one day..."

These thin threads of possibility held Laura together: a tenuous, fragile net. They were what allowed her to go through the motions. Showering. Walking to lessons. Changing for games. Changing back. Stumbling through the day. She couldn't eat anything because her stomach revulsed at it, but the others plied her with cups of tea.

By Saturday evening she was exhausted and went to bed again without managing to do any homework. By this time Grace Grant had called Charlotte in to "have a quiet word". Neither of them articulated Laura's actual loss though they both knew that each knew what it was. The housemistress spoke of a "difficult situation" and that she hoped Laura would feel a little better by Monday.

While Laura felt no better, the initial shock had worn off and she was getting used to the grief by the start of the next school week. The future seemed grey and bleak. She existed. Much of the time she wished she didn't.

28. Suffering

Of course Laura tried to call Mr Rydell. Incessantly. She only ever got through to Dean's answerphone though she never left a message.

After a week Dean finally picked up the phone. He hadn't been home, he had just come back from a work trip to discover his flatmate had cleared out leaving no forwarding address. A note said he'd taken "a leave of absence" from work.

"I've no idea where he's gone," Dean's tone was apologetic. "He had recently wrapped up one contract anyway, so maybe he'll resurface for the next one."

Laura half wished Dean was lying. At least it would mean she could keep pestering him until he gave her a number. But she could hear the genuine surprise and bewilderment in his voice.

"I truly am sorry, Laura. You both seemed so solid. I don't know what can be going on with him."

Laura thanked him, feeling even heavier than before. So that was that.

* * *

The others had rallied round in strong support. Margery took on the role of making sure Laura didn't stop eating, even slicing up Mars Bars and practically drip feeding them to her.

Susie sought Laura's help for assignments that she could have done perfectly well herself. But it kept Laura occupied. Left to her own devices she drifted off into tormented thoughts and imaginings. She kept wondering what Mr Rydell was up to and even whom he was with.

Charlotte took a different tactic. "Come running with me tomorrow morning."

Laura looked at Charlotte as though she were insane. "You mean your freezing cold, pitch dark self-torture? No way."

"You'll like it. It's so awful you'll enjoy it. It's like mortifying the flesh."

Despite herself, Laura agreed to give it a go. Anything to distract herself from thoughts of Mr Rydell. She had too much spirit to want to indulge her grief. She wanted the hurt to stop but it simply overwhelmed her.

Some girls might have wallowed in it, writing gloomy poems and weeping at rainy windows. But Laura knew, deep down, that this was futile. It wouldn't win him back. She needed a smarter campaign than that for she was determined not to give him up.

* * *

The next morning Laura regretted her whim to join Charlotte's running with every bone of her body. It was dark; her bed was warm. Outside the air was freezing. She was still tired. She wanted to curl up and go back to sleep. The alarm clock said six o'clock so they had at least another hour before they needed to rise. "Maybe another day…" she murmured but Charlotte had anticipated this.

A cold, wet cloth was dripped on her face and Laura started and jumped up, nearly yelling out loud and waking the others.

"It's time," said Charlotte, her torturer.

Laura hated putting on clothes without showering first but she pulled on tracksuit bottoms, a t-shirt and a tracksuit top. Charlotte had made her get her clothes together the previous night to avoid delay.

The two of them crept down the stairs of Michaelmas House as quietly possible and Charlotte carefully opened the front door. Matron unlocked it each morning at half past six so they could get back in on their return.

Outside the night air was so cold that it made Laura's chest tight. "You are going to go at my pace?" she asked Charlotte.

"Of course. I don't go that fast anyway."

Running around the dark playing fields, their feet crunching the frosted grass, it took some while for Laura's body heat to reach a level that counteracted the freezing air she was breathing in. It gave her a terrible cramp and she had to stop. "I've got a stitch," she called to Charlotte, as she bent double waiting for it to pass.

"You need to run through them."

"I can't, it's agony."

Charlotte jogged on the spot while she waited for Laura to recover. After that they got into a steady rhythm for the rest of the loop. The rhythm of their feet pounding on the ground started to take over.

Laura's thoughts were split between the discomforts of jogging and how far they had to go, and thoughts of Mr Rydell. She had the image of his face in her mind, always ahead of her.

How could Charlotte do this day after day? It was hell. Amazingly, Charlotte was able to hold a conversation while she jogged whereas Laura could barely catch her breath. She hadn't realised she was so unfit. Or maybe it was just that Charlotte was super fit.

"After the first lap you get into your stride and it's much easier," Charlotte said. "You feel like you could go on forever."

Laura wanted to refute this but couldn't manage to say anything. But she kept going. She found she enjoyed the companionship with Charlotte, the two of them alone in the dark pre-dawn world.

When they finally finished Laura was exhausted but exhilarated. "It would be pretty cool in a couple of months time when the sun is actually coming up," she said.

"Easier to get out of bed too. Except it won't be hockey season any more then, so I may not bother." Other sports such as tennis and athletics were played in summer.

Showering was also a revelation. After the steaming hot water washed off the cold sweat, Laura's limbs felt loose and silky. It wasn't enough inducement to make this a daily thing but it was some compensation.

* * *

For her own part, Laura focused on the dreaded Duke of Edinburgh expedition. Given her state of mind the grim ordeal of tramping over the moors in pouring rain carrying a heavy pack seemed no more bleak than not doing so.

Charlotte was too busy with hockey to bother with the route planning and Margery and Susie had no interest in it so it fell to Laura anyway. It made sense as she was the one with the surprise gift for orienteering.

So along with some of the other group leaders she went to the Geography classroom and pored over Ordnance Survey maps.

"You look very tired," Tom Hollier said to her one day. In just the few days since Mr Rydell had ended things Laura had lost weight and sleep. The morning runs with Charlotte temporarily boosted her colour for an hour or so, but by the afternoon it was apparent how little she had slept.

"That will be due to her dawn exercise," another girl from Michaelmas House told him. "She and Charlotte Bevan have become fitness freaks."

"Really?" The Geography teacher looked intrigued.

"Charlotte dragged me out running," Laura explained. "So I lost an hour of sleep." Thinking about it made her want to yawn. Her body felt brittle again, jagged, she longed to sink down onto a soft mattress and enjoy twelve hours of oblivion. But even a few hours were denied her, as dreams tormented her every night.

"I'm glad you're getting fit for Duke of Edinburgh," he said, "but don't overdo it."

Later that evening her dorm mates echoed the same sentiment.

"You do look exhausted, Laura." This was Margery.

"Thanks." Laura's tone was sarcastic though she knew it was true. She had even tried putting blusher on so Matron didn't start asking questions. She was longing for the end of term so she could get away from school for a while, from all the places that still reminded her of Mr Rydell.

* * *

Sometimes, despite her resolve, Laura still broke down. The worst time this happened was at the end of a route planning session. They were held at the end of the day when her energy and spirits sank lowest. Ahead lay supper, for which she had no appetite, and then yet another evening of homework and revision for mocks, hearing the phone ring for other girls but never for her.

Each time it shrilled up the stairway of Michaelmas House she couldn't stop feeling hope.

"Laura, I've changed my mind, I can't be without you." "I want you back." "I still love you."

But it was never him and each time the lead in her chest grew a little heavier.

She was so tired and sad that she was in a kind of daze looking down at her map, not even noticing she was the last to leave the room.

"Are you alright?" Tom Hollier had cleaned the blackboard and needed to leave.

Laura jerked her head up, causing the room to spin for a moment with flecks of static. She blinked. "I'm fine, it was just a long day."

He frowned. "You really don't look well at all. I think you should go to the school nurse."

Laura gave a weak smile. "It's not the kind of ailment she could fix."

Tom Hollier remembered how radiant she had been on Valentine's Day and guessed it might be teenage heartbreak. There wasn't a lot he could say. "If you do need to have a quiet moment, you can always use this classroom, it's often empty. I know it's a bit of a goldfish bowl here."

It was. Privacy was the rarest commodity at boarding school. Just like prison, Susie had once observed. Other than when using a bathroom cubicle you literally didn't get an inch of private space to yourself.

Laura saw the concern and sympathy in the Geography teacher's eyes and it made her own eyes well up with tears. She was okay with her friends showing sympathy, up to a point, but when it was someone like Tom Hollier or Grace Grant she lost it.

She dug her nails into her palms, willing herself to keep it together. "Thanks," she managed.

"If you're too sick for this expedition, you don't have to do it," he said.

But that would be admitting defeat. "I'll be alright."

And she would. Because she had to be.

29. Playing up

With all the drama over Laura's break up, Charlotte had put the stolen letter to the back of her mind. It was still in her history textbook, untouched. She felt unease at opening it because it wasn't addressed to her. Taking it was bad enough, but wasn't opening someone else's mail actually a postal crime?

In the end Charlotte asked Susie about it, figuring that Susie would manage to make her feel less guilty about it than Margery would. She didn't want to burden Laura at this time.

"Haven't you opened it yet? Why on earth not?" Susie was amused by Charlotte's qualms.

"It just feels like it's not really mine to open," Charlotte said.

Susie was crunching an apple. "It's not Grace Grant's either though, is it? She has no idea about any of this and isn't expecting a letter. If it morally belongs to anyone, it's Tony's aunt, given she masqueraded as Gi-Gi. I'm sure she wouldn't mind you opening it."

Charlotte was still uncertain so Susie increased the pressure.

"Do you want to model or don't you? This the tiniest detail. There'll be enough other obstacles ahead, why make it any harder on yourself?"

Although this was far from a convincing moral argument it spurred Charlotte into opening the dreaded envelope. To her relief all she found was a photocopy of the dual-signed contract, a welcome letter, and various pieces of information about the agency and what to expect.

"There you are you see. It's just bumpf. Gi-Gi wouldn't even be interested in it even if she had opened it, it would just go in a drawer. I mean if it was meant for her, of course," Susie tossed the apple core in a large arc and it landed perfectly in the centre of the wastepaper bin with a satisfying thud.

"Are you coming to breakfast?" Charlotte asked.

"That was breakfast. Because I need to stay back and finish this horrible calculus thing before Assembly. I'll see you later."

* * *

Charlotte should have put the envelope in a drawer. A locked drawer. But Susie's dismissal of its contents as "bumpf" lessened its sense of importance. It had felt like a Top Secret Dossier before, now it was just a form letter and some brochures.

So she stuffed it back inside Modern World History, a large and heavy book.

She was going to be late for breakfast herself if she didn't make haste, so she grabbed her things and hurried down to the common room. There she rapidly took out the books and folders she needed from her pigeon hole, stashed the ones she didn't want, and ran outside to try and avoid a demerit.

Somebody else was skipping breakfast that morning. That someone was Teresa Hubert, who also had homework to catch up on. She was sitting in the corner of the common room trying to finish it when Charlotte burst in and out, barely even noticing her.

But Teresa noticed Charlotte.

She also noticed that Modern World History was back on the shelf and she remembered Charlotte using it as a hiding place for her love letters or whatever they were. Was there anything juicy in it now, she wondered?

Bored with the essay she was supposed to be writing she decided to go and have a snoop. The pigeon holes were open to anyone but valuables were never kept there. It was also considered reasonable to briefly borrow someone else's text book so long as you didn't take it out of the room.

Regardless of the fact that her own copy of Modern World History was sitting in her own pigeon hole, Teresa felt quite justified in going and taking Charlotte's. She flicked through the pages and the letter immediately came to light.

At first Teresa was disappointed. It was clearly not a personal letter. She'd been hoping for something handwritten from a boy. Maybe even something compromising. Teresa herself had had minimal luck with boys so far which had made her extra resentful of Susie's and Charlotte's easy success with the cream of the crop of at St Duncan's.

Teresa noticed the logo and the business name. She frowned, recognising what it was: a modelling agency. A very famous one as well. She first assumed that Charlotte must have applied and that this was just information, shortly to be followed by an inevitable rejection. Anyway, the envelope had been opened so where was the harm in taking a peek?

She drew in her breath when she saw what it was. A contract of management! And with Charlotte's name on the cover, not a sample or anything. God, the girl would be simply unbearable. If it wasn't bad enough having to hear about Charlotte's oh-so-amazing hockey all the time, now they would all have to suffer endless tales of her brilliance on the catwalk. Not that Teresa thought Charlotte was anything special but she was very tall. That would be the only reason an agency could possibly have any interest in her.

Teresa knew that Charlotte's parents were strict and wondered if they knew. She suspected they did not. It might be a long shot, but maybe she could get this information to them somehow. Then if they didn't know, Charlotte would be in for a stormy Easter.

But what was this?

Her eyes narrowed as she found the cover letter: *"Dear Mrs Grant...."*

She looked again at the envelope and saw again the name of the intended recipient. *"Mrs G. Grant, Michaelmas House, 17 Hargate Road..."*

Now this was something!

Avidly, Teresa went through the contract, a sense of pleasure and triumph flooding through her veins. She found exactly what she was looking for. Someone had signed it as "Grace Grant" but it certainly wasn't their housemistress's handwriting or her signature. Just what was Charlotte up to?

Teresa had a damn good idea, but the question was what to do next. She was torn between wanting to see Grace Grant's reaction but not wanting to face a barrage of questioning. She could, she supposed, claim she had found the envelope on the floor. But this was so huge a matter that she wasn't sure if she really wanted her own name dragged into it. While she had every right to report this - in fact it was her duty, Teresa thought - being branded a "sneak" was not appealing.

So she took the easiest option. She put everything back into the envelope, re-sealed it as best she could with some sticky tape, and slipped it into the pile of mail outside the housemistress's study.

After all, she was only redirecting it to its rightful owner. No one could accuse her of doing anything wrong.

* * *

"How are you going to manage if the agency needs to call you during the holidays?" Laura asked Charlotte as they walked over to assembly. "Can you risk giving them your home number?"

Charlotte looked troubled. "Not really. I've been wondering what to do. I was hoping they might write, but I suppose if these casting calls come up at the last minute they'll need to phone. That's if I get anything, of course. They did say that nothing was guaranteed."

"You could give them my number," Margery said. "Tell them that you're temporarily staying at my address. Then I can call you with any messages."

"What happens if your father answers?" Laura asked.

"It won't matter, I don't think he'll mind. I mean he may mind, but I'm usually the one who answers the phone anyway. He hates getting calls, and we don't get too many."

This seemed a sad thing to say and Laura, amid her own desolation over Mr Rydell, felt a pang for Margery.

"That would be so cool if you could do that," Charlotte said.

Margery looked embarrassed but pleased. She had felt left out of many of the others' antics, albeit through her own choice, and this was a way that she could contribute.

"Do you need a chaperone for the castings?" Laura asked.

"I don't think so. If I was really young, like fourteen, then yes. But I think it's okay by now."

As they reached the chapel they could see Susie already there, chatting to Tom Hollier while she waited for them to arrive. Her face as usual was animated and her body language highly flirtatious, and the Geography teacher's was amused but wary.

"How did she get there so early?" Margery asked.

"She had to hand some homework in or something, before lessons," Charlotte told her.

"She skipped breakfast."

"That's because she was doing the homework then."

Susie, irrepressible, had spent the previous evening reading a novel rather than attending to her already-late History assignment. It was long overdue hence her last minute exertions. She greeted the others happily and Tom nodded to them.

"Mr Hollier was just informing me that if we fail this expedition we have to do it again next term, and miss the first exeat," Susie announced to them.

Charlotte looked at him in horror. "Is that true?"

"Absolutely. So try to avoid navigating yourselves to a country inn," he told them. "Or arranging to have some boyfriend meet you on the route and drive you to the campsite."

"Has someone actually done that?" Charlotte asked. She wished she had thought of it. Julian or Darius could easily have got access to a car and then they could have had an easy time of it. I'm turning into Susie, she thought. It was exactly the kind of plan Susie came up with.

"That, and worse. But they didn't get away with it and nor will you," Tom Hollier said.

Out of the corner of her eye Susie saw Mr Peters a few feet away. He was looking over at them all, specifically her. Deciding to have some fun she ran her tongue over her lips and looked up at Tom Hollier in the most ostentatiously provocative way possible.

"I think we could get away with anything, if we tried hard enough," she said, emphasising the word "hard". She knew Mr Peters was in earshot. Her body language was outrageous, arching up towards him and thrusting out her chest, almost a pantomime performance.

Laura, who could see Mr Peter's face, his lips tightly pursed but transfixed on Susie, guessed what her friend was up to and could barely stop laughing. Tom Hollier was in the dark but looked more bemused than concerned. He knew Susie's play-acting well enough by now to know that she wasn't serious.

"If you want to try Mrs Grayson's reaction, be my guest," he told her.

Susie tipped her head on one side and actually fluttered her eyelashes. "I'd love to be your guest."

In the background Mr Peters had gone puce. Laura had to turn away to hide her reaction, coughing to disguise her laughter.

"What's so funny?" Charlotte hissed at her.

"Mr Peters."

Charlotte hadn't noticed the English teacher watching Susie and Tom Hollier, and as soon as she did she simply burst out laughing. Tom Hollier looked at her quizzically. "Just something Laura said," Charlotte told him, at which Tom looked at Laura.

"It was nothing, sorry," she said.

The Geography teacher could tell something was going on but for now it was a mystery to him. He nodded over at his colleague before departing and was surprised to get a very tight and hostile nod in return. Tom Hollier had no idea of Mr Peters' ardour for Susie or that he had just made himself an enemy.

Susie's eyes were glinting as Tom Hollier left. The warning against misbehaving on the trip had sent the cogs of her mind spinning. Devilish ideas were already beginning to brew.

It was Margery who restrained her, after Tom Hollier had left.

"Let's just do this one properly. I really don't want to have another trip hanging over my head all Easter, next term is going to be bad enough as it is."

Susie perceived Margery's anguish. It would take the fun out of misbehaving to know that Margery was stressing out. "Okay then. We'll be perfect little expeditioners. But we really do have to find some kind of way for you to have fun, Margie."

* * *

Despite his pique Mr Peters was even more unctuous towards Susie in English later that day. They had finished Under Milk Wood and were fully in revision mode for mocks. Mr Peters was taking them through some essay questions on Twelfth Night from previous examination papers.

"Describe three points at which the comic subplots intersect with the main plot," Mr Peters said. "That theme came up a few years ago. You'll almost certainly get a question on disguise or inversion, and most likely one on romantic themes." His eyes flicked briefly to Susie and back as he said this.

Someone put up their hand to ask what was meant by intersect, and Laura found herself gazing at some of Shakespeare's lines:

A contract of eternal bond of love,
Confirm'd by mutual joinder of your hands,
Attested by the holy close of lips

The verse took her back to the first time Mr Rydell had ever kissed her. Illicitly in his classroom just as the day was fading.

She remembered how it had almost felt sacred. From the moment his lips met hers she had belonged to him, completely. It could never be undone.

She knew he had felt the same. Although she had had doubts and insecurities she had always been aware at some level of the intensity of his feelings for her. That couldn't just ebb away, could it? If you were angry enough or disappointed enough with someone, as she feared he had been with her, and you tried to forget them, could it happen?

Laura's reverie was disrupted by a sharp nudge from Margery, who indicated Mr Peters. He had asked her a question.

"I'm sorry, what was it?"

Mr Peters repeated the question, his expression highly displeased. Laura managed to stumble out an answer that fortunately satisfied him as it was his own theory that he had previously shared with them. That was the problem, you always got the best marks by writing what teachers wanted to hear, not what you actually thought.

30. Expedition

"Mould and mildew and misery."

This was Charlotte's verdict on the huge, smelly canvas tents they were required to carry on the Duke of Edinburgh Award expedition.

"You can get those little lightweight tents now," Charlotte continued. "These look like something left over from World War One."

They were two-person tents which meant that one person had to carry them, and the other had to carry half of their gear to compensate. Their backpacks had seemed heavy enough without this added burden.

"They really do stink, don't they?" Margery said.

It seemed an awful lot of baggage for a single night's camping. Everyone was required to carry a full change of clothes, waterproofs, a sleeping bag and cooking equipment. Laura couldn't see why it wasn't possible to just take some chocolate bars, but they were made to take actual ration packs.

These contained small stoves that ran on solid fuel blocks as well as cooking containers, which being made of metal added even more weight. Laura grimaced as she read the contents. "Porridge oats, canned bacon and something called 'biscuits brown'. Thank God it's only for one night."

"I feel we may actually be going to fight a war," Susie said. "The whole D of E thing is a cover and we're instead being sent to the front lines."

This was said in earshot of Tom Hollier, deliberately for him to overhear.

"Whom do you imagine you'll be fighting?" he asked.

"Cornwall, probably. They're always trying to secede," Charlotte said. "Or Scotland."

Tom laughed. "It's clear you don't do Geography."

"If we die of exposure on the moors, will you build us a memorial?" Susie asked. "One of those stone cairns would be nice."

"I'm sure it can be arranged."

* * *

It was a long trudge over bleak, hilly terrain after they finally set off. Margery was the least fit so they made frequent stops to let her catch her breath after uphill stretches.

"Are you actually getting a thing for Tom?" Charlotte asked Susie.

"Not in a million years."

"I sometimes wonder if he's getting a thing for you," Charlotte said.

"Not in a millions years that either. You really don't have to worry," Susie told her. "We are just friends. Anyway I can tell what his type is and it's not me, and nor is he my type."

Margery was secretly relieved to hear this. The thought of another one of her friends crossing the student-teacher line was too much to contemplate.

"It's going to be freezing tonight," Laura said. Their sleeping bags were supposedly insulated but she feared their noses would get cold. And if you rolled over it would doubtless send sharp darts of icy air straight down inside.

"We'll light a fire," Susie said.

Charlotte looked intrigued. "Are we allowed to do that?" she asked, forgetting momentarily that the question of permission meant absolutely nothing to Susie.

"We haven't got any firewood," Margery said.

"Not to worry. We'll find a thicket or a coppice or a grove," Susie said. "Laura surely knows the map symbols."

Laura had no idea if a symbol for a thicket existed, but she figured a green tree symbol was probably near enough. "We'll see trees if they're in range," she pointed out. One advantage to trudging up these endless hills was that you did get a good view of the surrounding landscape.

"Not if it's dark," Charlotte pointed out.

"We're supposed to be at the camp well before nightfall. If we're much later they send out a search party," Laura told her.

Their backs and shoulders aching from the heavy packs and blisters rubbing against their walking boots, the four of them trudged on. The grass was thick and damp and spongey and certain parts squelched to tread on. The trek was far less interesting than the orienteering since it was just endless hiking. Laura barely even needed to map read: the route was so straightforward and Tom had prepared them all so well.

She could see that Margery was starting to struggle. "Shall we take a few minutes rest and have a drink?" she suggested.

Margery sank down with relief. She was starting to think she couldn't make it. Her feet were throbbing in agony. She felt as though she would never be able to stand again until Charlotte exclaimed "Look! A massive slug!" and Margery jumped up with a shriek, nearly spilling all her water.

"God it really is huge," Susie said, peering at it. "I hope they don't get inside the tents."

* * *

The campfire generated more smoke than heat as most of the wood they had found was damp. It was a strangely primaeval feeling sitting on top of the moors, the sky ink-black above and the smell of damp grass and wood smoke winding around them.

They sipped a syrupy black tea boiled up on a hexamine stove. "It's like being gypsies," Charlotte said. "It's quite romantic, isn't it?"

"Until a storm blows the tents over," Laura said. She saw a light in the distance, moving around. "What's that?"

"A ghost?"

"Someone with a torch."

"A murderer, then."

It turned out to be Tom Hollier who was making an inspection of all the campsites, which were all pitched over the same square mile or so of moorland. "How are you all doing? Guy ropes secure?"

"You nearly gave us a heart attack coming up in the dark," Susie told him.

He grinned, his face illuminated by the storm lantern he had set down. "I would have made it before nightfall but we've had some hiccups with some of the tents. Yours seem fine though," he said as he tested the ropes.

"Are we in for storms?" Charlotte asked.

"Not tonight. Well, if you're all set, I'll be on my way." He made to leave.

"We can't tempt you with a hot cup of tea?" Susie offered.

He hesitated. "Seeing as you're the last on my round."

Laura poured him the remains of the tea from the small metal pan they had used to boil it up in. It was square with a folding handle. He tasted it and grimaced. "Sure you've got enough sugar in here? It's like treacle."

"It was really bitter otherwise," Charlotte explained.

"It's a good fire. Who built it?" he asked.

"Laura."

"We have bonfires on the beach all the time back home," Laura explained. "In summer anyway."

"That must be nice. Cornwall isn't it?"

"Yes, it is nice, but it's far," Laura said. She wondered what the time was. She thought it had been dark for at least a couple of hours but it was hard to judge time in this place. If she knew more about the moon and how it moved across the sky she could probably have worked it out since it was a clear night. The moon was nearly full. Gibbous, she vaguely recalled.

"Where are you from?" Charlotte asked Tom.

"Cheshire," he told her.

"You don't have much of an accent."

"I didn't really grow up there. I went to boarding school down south," he explained.

Susie laughed. "Institutionalised, just like us."

"I don't think even a maximum security prison could institutionalise you," he said drily.

It was strange having a conversation in the dark. You couldn't see people's faces very well, mainly the shine of their eyes. Laura was glad to be there, away from it all. Somewhere with no reminders of the person she was missing. Of course she thought about him, constantly, but being out here she finally felt as though she could breathe.

She was on top of the world and he was someone out there, and she would find him. She vowed that she would find him.

Eventually Tom left them, double checking their tent was secure.

"It's so freezing I almost would, you know," Susie said after he had gone. She poked the fire with a stick.

"Would what?" Margery asked.

"Have let him in my tent," Susie said. "Solely to keep warm, of course."

"Me too," Charlotte said. "He looked really fit in the firelight."

"I don't think he was offering," Margery said.

"Oh he would have, I'm sure," Susie replied. "With the right invitation."

Laura only wanted one person to warm her in her tent. But he could be anywhere in the world. Anywhere under this vast, dark sky with its cold and distant stars.

Inside the tent it stank of damp canvas and mildew. It would take weeks of drying out in hot sunny weather for the fabric to even start to become pleasant, but tonight was chill and dewy. It kept the wind off: that was about all you could say for it.

"Time to bunker down then," Susie said. "If I snore, feel free to poke me." She never snored.

"Goodnight." Laura adjusted the lumpen pillow she had fashioned out of a t-shirt stuffed with spare clothes and hoped sleep would come quickly.

31. Found out

"Charlotte, could you please come and see me when you have showered and changed."

Grace Grant's tone was uncharacteristically grave on their return to Michaelmas House. Susie and Laura exchanged a worried glance.

"I knew something awful was going to happen," Margery was fretting as they climbed the stairs. "I just knew it. It's all been far too risky."

"We don't know anything yet," Laura told her, seeing how stressed Charlotte was looking. They had been on something of a knife edge with the endless subterfuge over the modelling agency. All except Susie who only thrived on such tension.

Charlotte barely spoke as she quickly washed and pulled clean clothes on. She felt sick to her stomach.

"It will be okay," Susie said. "It's not like you've done anything really terrible. You haven't committed a crime or done something unforgivable, like cheat in an exam."

They all felt for her. The look on Grace Grant's face was one that no one ever wanted to see.

Charlotte went down the stairs feeling as though she were approaching her execution. She knocked on the housemistress's door.

"Come in."

Charlotte entered and was instructed to take a seat. This was a very slim relief since if you had done something catastrophic you were usually made to stand.

Grace Grant held up the envelope from the modelling agency. Charlotte started, recognising it immediately. "Would you care to explain this?"

There was nothing for it but to come clean and play it as straight as possible.

"It's from a modelling agency."

"That is quite clear. What I would like to know is why it is addressed to me, and more seriously, why my name has been signed to a legal contract on your behalf?"

Charlotte gripped the seat of the chair she was sitting on. How on earth had Grace Grant got hold of the letter? It had been in her history textbook, hidden. Who had found it? Had it dropped out? She was kicking herself for not locking it in her trunk or destroying it.

"I didn't think they were going to write to you," she said.

"That much is clear. Perhaps you had better start from the beginning."

So Charlotte tried her best. She gave as true an account as possible, changing a few details to disguise the fact that they'd spent an exeat weekend in London. Instead she implied that it had all happened in half term, which meant she needed to pretend it had been with Margery as she had stayed with her during half term. So she ran the first two events together - the approach by Barbara Banks and the initial appointment - since Margery had been there for the latter.

"I didn't know what to do. I thought my parents would freak out, but it said you needed a guardian. And when we're here at school, well there's the loco parentis thing, so I thought from a legal point of view..."

"Except that I didn't actually sign this, did I? So it is completely void in the eyes of the law. Do you realise how serious it is to forge a signature on a legal document?"

"It wasn't actually me who signed it," Charlotte mumbled.

"Then exactly who did sign it? One of your dormitory members?"

"No, it was someone's aunt." Charlotte blushed just thinking about the contrast between Tony's Pearly Queen auntie and the housemistress. It would be beyond ghastly if Grace Grant ever found out who had impersonated her.

Grace Grant sighed. Charlotte expected her to look angry but she looked more worried. "Why did you do this, Charlotte? It seems very out of character for you."

"I just wanted to try the modelling so badly. And I knew my parents would never consent. And it's not like it's much longer before I could sign the contract for myself anyway," Charlotte said. She tried to explain. "It's not that I want to be a model long term or anything, for a career. I want to finish school, go to university. Play hockey most of all. But doing this for now would give me, you know, choices."

The housemistress understood what the girl was trying to say. She had met the domineering Mr Bevan on a few occasions and had every sympathy for any girl who had a father like him. She was also conscious that the faked signature, albeit extremely foolish, was not the equivalent of forging a cheque. Nor had any real offence been committed on school grounds. But she still had her responsibilities.

"Your parents will have to be told, I'm afraid."

Charlotte looked up at her, pleading. "They'll go mad. My father will probably withdraw me from school or something." She'd never get to play hockey ever again. The thought filled her with black misery.

Grace Grant picked up the offending documents and glanced over them again. "You're usually such an exemplary pupil. Your grades are very good, you've worked exceptionally hard at your hockey, you usually manage to stay out of trouble. Because of this I'm going to let you do the right thing and tell your parents, and get them to write to me with their response. If you can do this by the start of next term then I won't take it any further. Otherwise…"

She didn't continue but they both knew how serious it would be if Charlotte didn't sort it out.

"I'll do my best," Charlotte said.

"I know you will."

* * *

The four of them sat around the dorm in an atmosphere of doom and gloom.

"Maybe you can get through to your parents somehow," Laura was saying. "After all the photos are beautiful. They would surely be proud of you."

She knew it was hopeless even as she said it.

"I suppose in the absolute worst case scenario you could just wait until you can legally sign, and do it then," Margery suggested.

"By then I'll be geriatric by modelling standards," Charlotte said.

Thus far Susie hadn't said anything. She was sitting cross-legged on top of her bed in her usual fashion and Laura could see that the cogs of her mind were turning.

Finally she spoke. "The only two things Gi-Gi picked you up on were not telling your parents and forging her signature. Obviously you didn't tell her about any of the exeat stuff. But what about you taking the letter and opening it? Going through her mail would also be a pretty major offence."

"She didn't mention that," Charlotte said.

"But she must have known. Even if she didn't notice the postal stamp date, she would have seen that the letter was opened. So it would have been obvious that you or someone else had taken it."

Charlotte hadn't really thought about this detail since what had happened was overwhelming enough.

Susie continued. "It's possible that someone found it, saw her name and put it back in the pile as though it had come in with her other mail. But it would obviously look tampered with. Don't you think she would be curious about that?"

A little detail was flickering in Charlotte's mind. Tape. Tape on the edge of the envelope as Grace Grant had drawn the contract out.

"There was Sellotape on it," she said, frowning. "But I'm sure there wasn't before. You remember, we opened it in here. I only remember glue."

"Maybe someone resealed it for privacy's sake?" Laura suggested. "If they were putting it back on her table, perhaps they thought it was safer?"

Susie wasn't satisfied. "It all seems very odd to me. And when and how did they find it in the first place? I saw you put it back in that book on Friday morning, then we were off camping on Saturday morning. You haven't used your history book in that time."

They all tried to figure out how it could have fallen out. "I carried it straight to my pigeon hole," Charlotte said.

"Maybe it fell on the stairs on the way?"

Charlotte thought back to that morning. "No, because I was clamping it shut as I carried it."

"So someone must have taken your book from your pigeon hole to find that letter. There's something really deliberate about all the Sellotaping and slipping it back to Gi-Gi. Someone intentionally set you up and I bet I know who. Did you see anyone around the common room when you were in there?"

"Not that I remember, but I was in a huge rush."

"Well I did. About ten minutes after you left I saw Teresa Hubert rushing along the path towards school."

There was silence as everyone digested it.

"We've got no proof it was her," Laura said.

Margery had thought of something. "You remember when you first showed us that letter, a week or so ago in history? I do remember Teresa leaning over and trying to see. She looked very curious."

"Ten to one it's that vile sneaky bitch," Charlotte said. "But what do we do?"

Susie smiled. "You leave Teresa to me. I'll deal with her. But you need to figure out telling your parents."

Charlotte put her head in her hands. She was in despair about that. "What the hell am I going to do?"

"You're going to pray that a casting comes up and you manage to get a paid job before the end of the holidays," Susie told her. "Only then do you tell your parents. You have five weeks."

"And if that doesn't happen?"

"You keep quiet and wait until they are driving you back to school next term. Just as you are getting out of the car with your trunk and everything, you mention it. If your father explodes at least there will be dozens of witnesses."

32. A clue

Laura tried ringing Dean again in the final week of term. She waited for a time when there was nobody around which was difficult.

Alone, in the silence and dimness of the corridor, she prayed silently for news. Anything. Just a grain of hope.

"Laura, hi. I'm afraid I haven't heard anything."

She was expecting this but the disappointment still twisted in her gut. The world seemed duller again. "Thanks anyway. I guess I wanted to know if he was okay." And if he missed her. And if he had changed his mind. And if he wanted her back.

Dean was silent for a moment. "There is one thing. Some mail arrived for him which I opened in case it was urgent. It was from Brookfields & Haigh - a letting agency - asking him to confirm if he wants them to find new tenants for his house. The lease is up in July apparently and the current tenants don't wish to renew. It didn't include an address or I would have forwarded it onto there."

Even Mr Rydell's agents didn't know where he was. How could he just disappear like that? If only she knew more of his friends, of his family. Some way to trace him. But it was hopeless.

"Anyway," Dean continued, "I've called the agency to say he's no longer at this address but if you do hear from him, you might let him know."

Laura felt a tiny bit encouraged by Dean's suggestion that Mr Rydell might still get in touch with her. Though she herself thought it unlikely. She was losing hope.

* * *

Later that day Laura mentioned the call to Susie who instantly perked up. "Mr Rydell owns a house? Haven't you tried there?"

"I don't know where it is, and he doesn't even live there," Laura said. "It's rented out. I don't think he's ever lived there."

"But the letting agency must know where it is. What were they called?"

By then Laura could barely remember. "Rockfields or something. It was two words."

Susie rolled her eyes. "Try to remember. We can probably try the Yellow Pages as well. And do you know what county it's in, at least?"

"It's in Hampshire somewhere. I could call Dean again."

"Do that," Susie told her. "Then you can find out the address."

"You mean just call them and ask them?"

"God no! They won't just give out information like that unless you're the police or something. Although I suppose we could try Land Registry, but that's the other way round. You need the address to find out the owner. There's also the Electoral Roll, but if he hasn't lived there ever it probably has another address for him which may be really old," Susie said.

"How do you know all this stuff?"

Susie grinned and tried to look mysterious. "You never know when you might need to track someone down."

Laura was still thinking about the lettings agency. "It might have been Brookdale. Or Brookfield. Something like that."

"We'll look for all the ones that start with Brook and Rock then, and you'll probably recognise it. There can't be that many," Susie said.

Laura was still in the dark about Susie's plan. "So what do we do then?"

"We ring them and say that we're looking to lease a house in Hampshire, from July, and do they have anything on their books."

"And then?"

"Then they'll probably send you a list of properties in the area, including his house," Susie said. "But we should do it soon before they either find a new tenant or he tells them he doesn't want to find one. Depending on what his plans are."

But what if the list was really long? "How will we know which one it is?"

"We'll have to do some detective work. I'll help. And we'll try the electoral roll as well, you never know, it might have his parents' address on it," Susie said.

Finding his address was a goal at least even if it led nowhere in the end. The way Mr Rydell had gone out of contact with Laura had made her realise how isolated their relationship had been. They hadn't met one another's families, for obvious reasons. Dean was the only friend she had ever met of his. Her parents had no idea he even existed.

Somehow, if she ever did manage to find him again, that would have to change.

* * *

Finally the term came to a close and everyone was rushing off for the Easter holidays. It should have been a time of excitement: four weeks of holidays, then when they came back they could start looking forward to summer.

But they were all very worried for Charlotte. Margery planned to help out where she could and have Charlotte to stay if she needed to go up to London. They all knew it was going to be hopeless with Charlotte's father, whatever the outcome.

"I don't blame Gi-Gi," Charlotte said. "She's been as reasonable as she can be, given the circumstances." She was stuffing the last of her things into her trunk. Things never fitted at the end of term, even though Margery was hiding the nightclub dress and shoes for her.

"I do blame Teresa," Susie said. She was working on getting proof one way or the other, and when she did, Teresa would wish she had never been born.

Laura couldn't help thinking about how far Cornwall was from London and all the other places that Mr Rydell might be. At least Susie was coming to stay with her the week after Easter. It was something to look forward to.

Then Margery surprised everyone. "You know, you could just do it anyway," she said to Charlotte.

"Do what?"

"The modelling thing. Tell your father about the approach from an agency, he'll obviously go off his head. Tell Grace Grant that he's forbidden you from doing it, or get a letter from him, whatever. Then just do it. You've signed the contract after all. If they call you, just go up to London and don't tell anyone. Except us of course, so we can help."

"Margery!" Charlotte was shocked.

Even Susie was taken aback. "Where did this change of heart come about?"

Margery shrugged. "It's not really a change of heart. I've always thought the modelling was a good idea." She knew Charlotte's father better than any of them and had long worried about the future battles Charlotte might face when it came to university. "There's nothing wrong with it. When I went to the agency it seemed really professional and they have all those famous models. It's not like you're going to be on Page Three, is it?" she said to Charlotte.

They were all excited now.

"What if my father ends up seeing photos of me somewhere?"

"If you end up on a billboard you'll probably be getting so much money that the whole situation will be different," Susie said. "Margie it's a great idea. And we'll all do what we can to help."

Margery looked pleased and embarrassed by their reactions. "Of course you can always stay at mine whenever you need to go up to London. Any of you," she said.

"Is this the new rebellious, rule-breaking Margery?" Susie asked.

"Not really. I just think it would be a waste of an opportunity otherwise. And if you do get famous and see those guys again," Margery said to Charlotte, "you can get me their autographs."

"We can do better than that. You can come and meet them or whatever other celebrities Charlotte starts hanging out with," Susie said.

"Not in an exam term, but thanks anyway," Margery said.

Susie smiled to herself. She had her own plans for next term. A slightly different style of plan than before but one that would be no less diverting. She had no doubt that she could pull it off.

Anything she set her mind to, she could succeed at. It was only a matter of planning and tenacity.

* * *

Laura took the train home which gave her a long time to think about everything that had happened to her that term. From Italy through half-term to the stress over the pregnancy scare and that final, terrible phone call.

The funny thing was that despite everything, despite all the things she had realised and the imperfections she had recognised in her relationship, one thing was now clearer to Laura than anything.

She loved Mr Rydell, deeply, honestly and absolutely.

She fingered the diamond he had given her that she still wore about her neck. It was the safest place for it and felt like her only link to him. Sometimes she felt that she didn't have a right to wear it any more.

"I hope this will be on a ring one day," he had said to her. It seemed so long ago now.

She had thought at the time that he had meant it. That they were forever.

Laura took the necklace off and dangled it in the light of the window. The jewel glittered: small but resilient. Unchanging. Permanent.

Do you still love me? Have you forgotten me? Do you think about me and miss me?

As young and inexperienced as she might be, Laura knew herself well enough to know that her love for him would never change.

So she would be patient. Wait out the school year, as Susie advised. And then if she still felt the same - for she knew she would - she would find him.

Some things were meant to be. And she was meant to be with him. Heart, body and soul.

* * *

201

About Noël Cades

Noël Cades is a British writer who currently lives in Sydney, Australia. A fan of romance from historic to erotic, some of Noël's favourite authors include Jilly Cooper, Jackie Collins, Elizabeth Rolls and Victoria Holt.

Noël is always delighted to hear from other fans, readers and writers of romance.

You can contact Noël at noelcades@gmail.com

Noël's website is at http://www.noelcades.com

Visit Noël's blog to sign up for exclusive news and the chance to receive new free book giveaways.

Excerpts from Summer's Edge by Noël Cades

Alice remained silent throughout this. She was still feeling disappointed and uncertain. She tried to tell herself it was for the best. Really, she should be grateful that he had just decided to move past it.

But she still felt embarrassed. She picked at the grass next to her, pulling off a small flower, avoiding looking at the play.

Then a shadow fell over them. She looked up.

It was Mr Walker.

"I want a word with you. In the pavilion, now," he ordered her. His eyes pierced into hers and he looked furious.

Numb, she obeyed, walking ahead of him.

Inside it was empty and he closed the door behind them and turned to her.

"What the fuck do you think you're playing at?"

He was absolutely incensed. He stood there, suddenly the adult, the authority, not just some guy she had kissed in a pub.

Someone she had compromised. Alice couldn't think of anything to say.

She stood there in front of him. His scent of faint cologne and sun-warmed skin was disturbingly familiar to her, mingling with the dusty wood and sports equipment smell of the pavilion.

"Did you know who I was?" he asked.

"Yes." There didn't seem to be any point in lying.

He glared at her and she looked back at him. His eyes pierced into her, their light grey-blue contrasting with his tanned complexion. He was one of the most devastatingly attractive men she had ever seen. All the more so now as his anger turned his face into carved steel.

As terrified and awkward as Alice felt, she also felt slightly defiant. After all she hadn't done anything wrong or illegal.

Then suddenly he grasped her by the shoulders and brought his mouth down on hers, hard. Surprised, she initially squirmed to escape his grasp then yielded as her forced his tongue into her mouth. His lips were bruising hers, he was almost biting her yet she wanted more.

Her hands, which had pushed against his chest to try and get away, went round his neck and she arched against him.

He was trying to hurt her, devour her. Punish her. All at once. But he wanted her too. She could taste his need, raw and urgent. Feel the hotness of his breath as he nearly suffocated her with his kiss.

His mouth left hers and moved to her neck, half embracing, half biting it. She tasted blood on her lip where he had crushed it with his own. He was gripping her hard and she clung to him. She didn't even care that he was hurting her.

He could have ripped all her clothes off right there and forced himself upon her. She had never wanted anyone so much.

Then just as suddenly he thrust her away from him. He swore under his breath as he tried to recover himself.

"Is that what you wanted?"

"No… yes… I mean…" Alice had no idea what to say. She was shaken and half in misery, half in ecstasy.

His face was like granite, its angles unyielding.

"Get out and don't come back here again. Stay out of my way," he said.

* * *

Alice tried to enjoy herself at the barbecue but she couldn't relax with Mr Walker just metres away, deliberately avoiding her. She had no appetite but knew she needed to eat something to avoid getting completely drunk on an empty stomach.

Graeme was good company and buoyed up by misery, alcohol and perhaps a desire to make a point to Mr Walker she flirted with him a bit. He was the kind of guy you could flirt with without it meaning much. Besides she knew he preferred Jules. She also noticed that Mr Walker's gaze was frequently on her and he didn't look happy about her flirting with Graeme. Or she hoped that was why he looked annoyed.

As the beer went down the revelry increased and someone accidentally knocked a glass full of beer over Alice. It went all over her top.

Feeling as though nothing much more could go wrong with the day she found her way to the kitchen and tried to sponge out the worst at the sink. If the beer dried on it, it would smell awful and probably stain the fabric. Hopefully even though she was getting her top even more wet it would dry quickly in the sun.

As she was finishing getting the worst off someone else came into the kitchen. She knew even before she turned that it was Mr Walker. He looked angry.

"Did you come here deliberately?" he asked.

She faced him. "I came here with Becky. I didn't know you'd be here. Or care," she added.

"What have you done to your shirt?"

"Someone spilt beer on it. I was washing it off."

"You can't go back out like that. You look like a wet t-shirt competition," he told her.

Alice looked down and went red. The wet fabric had gone transparent and soaked through her bra too.

Without a word Mr Walker pulled off his own shirt and handed it to her. He wore nothing under it. Alice was transfixed by his physique. His arms rippled with muscle and his flat, hard chest was tanned a deep gold. He was far fitter than she expected a cricketer to be, really powerful looking.

"Put this on."

The shirt was white cotton and warm from his body. She held it. It smelt of him. She wanted to envelop herself in it but she didn't follow his order.

"You want me to walk out of here wearing your shirt with you following me, topless?" she asked him.

He was silent for a moment, glaring at her. She was right, it would have exactly the opposite effect he intended. The situation was bad enough as it was.

"I don't want them gawping at you."

Alice's stomach gave a secret flip. Possessive and protective. He clearly didn't feel as neutrally towards her as he wanted to.

"The sun will dry it. I'll cross my arms." As she said this, she deliberately left her arms uncrossed and put her shoulders back slightly.

It had the desired effect. He was momentarily transfixed.

"Jesus Christ."

Alice took charge of the situation. "You should put this back on." Instead of just handing it to him she went to put it over his head meaning her arms were raised and her body was nearly against his. He was still for a second before taking a step backwards. A muscle clenched in his jaw.

"Just give me the shirt." She did so and he put it back on.

Then they both stood there. The tension was unbearable. She knew he wanted her and was fighting against it with every fibre of his being.

She broke the ice. "I am sorry you know. We were all just having fun the other night and I just didn't think about the implications."

"You were just messing around with me because I'm employed at your school?"

"God no, that wasn't why." Alice couldn't believe he thought this. Surely he'd realised how much she also wanted him to kiss her that night?

"So even if I hadn't been, you would have still put on your little act?" he asked.

What act? "I wasn't acting, I genuinely..."

"You wanted it too?"

"Yes." It was barely a whisper.

For a moment she thought he was going to kiss her again. He was wavering. Then he stood straighter. "I'm way too old for you, Alice, and I work at your school. Get back outside."

To find out what happens between Alice and Mr Walker, read Noël Cades' thrilling taboo student-teacher romance, Summer's Edge.

www.ingramcontent.com/pod-product-compliance
Lightning Source LLC
Chambersburg PA
CBHW030523020726
47494CB00004B/1207